Norman Murray

Illustrated guide to Montreal

Norman Murray

Illustrated guide to Montreal

ISBN/EAN: 9783742832832

Manufactured in Europe, USA, Canada, Australia, Japa

Cover: Foto ©Andreas Hilbeck / pixelio.de

Manufactured and distributed by brebook publishing software
(www.brebook.com)

Norman Murray

Illustrated guide to Montreal

Presented to
Albert Britnell Esq
with the authors compliments
and best wishes

New Year 1892
from

Norman Murray

May our business relations
long continue as they have
been since the commencement

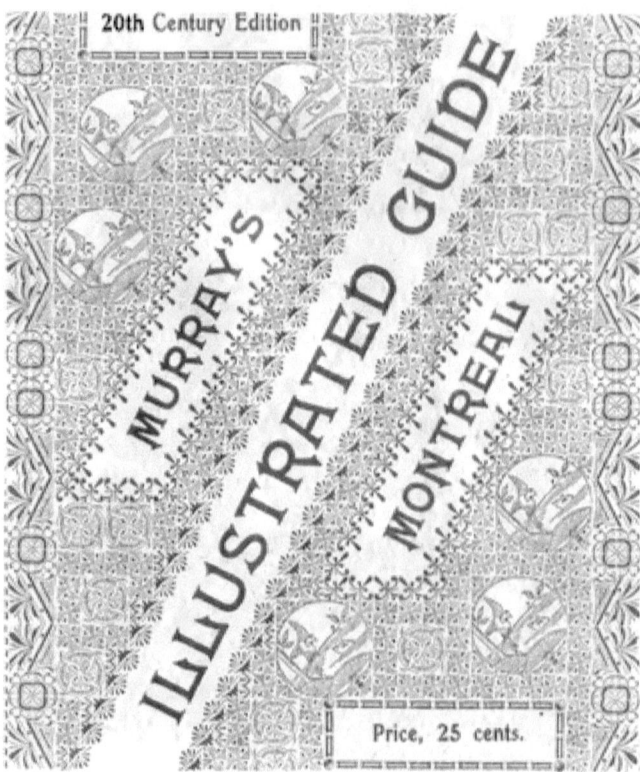

20th Century Edition

MURRAY'S

ILLUSTRATED GUIDE

MONTREAL

Price, 25 cents.

..ay English Morning Daily in Montreal
the Oldest Newspaper in the Dominion.

(ESTABLISHED 1778)

The Gazette

. . RETAINS ITS POSITION AS . .

The Leading Journal of the Province in Character,
Standing and Influence.

Fullest Cable and Telegraphic News,

Exclusive and Reliable Financial News,

Authoritative Market Reports,

Impartial Reports of Sports,

Trustworthy Shipping Intelligence

. . IN . .

THE GAZETTE.

ADDRESS ORDERS———

RICHARD WHITE,
Managing Director,
MONTREAL.

In all homes in all the Provinces of Canada, the universal favorite family newspaper is the ⚘ ⚘

(M)ontreal Star

IT GOES EVERYWHERE,
IS READ EVERYWHERE,
AND IS LIKED EVERYWHERE.

Never in the history of British North America has there been such a newspaper success as the STAR. Its supremacy is fully and freely acknowledged by all the other first-class newspapers of Canada.

PREFACE.

✄ ✄ ✄

There is a long distance between a poor crofter's fireside at the Butt of Lewis and writing up the Montreal of the beginning of the twentieth century. Every true man loves his native land and the land of his adoption. As I look back on the past, with all its struggles and wanderings on sea and land, it would be very ungrateful of me not to acknowledge the kindness of the people of Montreal in general to myself. For fifteen years we have discussed religion and politics from various points of view. I have become personally acquainted with people of various nationalities, with various views, on various subjects, and with the exception of a few isolated instances, where they were least to be expected, I have received the most kindly treatment, often where an ordinary observer would least expect. I venture to say that a stranger making his abode in a strange city is the best of all judges of the character of its people. Many of the people who helped me to earn my living for so many years are mentioned in this book.

Many more alas are gone to the other side, and many I don't even know their names, their nationality, religion or politics. If I get my wish, and end my days in a cottage of my own in the Island of Lewis, and a Montrealer wanders that way, I won't ask him whether he's a Jew or Gentile, Protestant or Catholic. If he has ever been in Montreal, he will be a welcome guest.

> As it is only lately I discovered I could rhyme,
> I think I'll try and give you my impressions of the time ;
> I would be most ungrateful if I neglected Montreal,
> So in my memorandum I'll put it first of all.

> It is a noble city—no better in the land ;
> I'll prefer it to any other while I'm above the sand,
> And though we do at times each other criticise,
> This is always a privilege true Britons exercise.

But to study human nature there's no place here below,
Where there's more variety of different kinds to show.
Sometimes you hear smart people say that we are slow,
So great and mighty rivers slow oftentimes do flow.

I have come here a stranger—did not know a man in town—
There are very few now in the city know more up and down ;
And though I have no riches of which I can boast,
Still, here's to old Montreal, I'll give her the first toast.

We have English, French and Irish, Scotchmen and some Jews,
We have Germans and Italians and several other crews,
We have socialists and anarchists, some tories and some whigs,
But for a party as a party I would not give two figs.

And sometimes in the summer we have Yankees from the States,
And we always like to see them for they are mostly first class mates :
And though we think sometimes that they blow a little high,
We can stand it all and more, and wink the other eye.

Do you know I rather like the man that sticks up for his own,
But I have no use for anyone who does his own disown,
And though sometimes I rub them (it's only just for fun)
I don't wish any harm to one below the sun.

And though in matters of religion we often disagree,
Your theories and dogmas are indifferent to me ;
And though I don't like Moses and old David would displace,
I think the MAN OF GALILEE the greatest of the race.

Bank of Montreal

ESTABLISHED 1817.

INCORPORATED BY ACT OF PARLIAMENT.

Capital (*all paid up*), - - - - - $12,000,000
Reserved Fund, - - - - - - - 7,000,000
Undivided Profits, - - - - - - 764,703

HEAD OFFICE, MONTREAL.

Board of Directors :

RT. HON. LORD STRATHCONA AND MOUNT ROYAL, G.C.M.G., PRESIDENT.
HON. G. A. DRUMMOND, VICE-PRESIDENT.

A. T. PATERSON, Esq.   R. B. ANGUS, Esq.
E. B. GREENSHIELDS, Esq.   A. F. GAULT, Esq.
SIR WILLIAM C. MACDONALD.   JAMES ROSS, Esq.
          R. G. REID, Esq.

E. S. CLOUSTON, GENERAL MANAGER.

BANK OF MONTREAL.— *Continued.*

LIABILITIES AND ASSETS.

30th April, 1901.

LIABILITIES.

Notes in Circulation...	$ 6,482,214
Deposits...	72,683,627
	$79,168,841

ASSETS.

Specie and Dominion Notes	$ 6,036,796
Due by other Banks and Foreign Agents	4,800,424
Call and short Loans in Great Britain and United States	23,536,028
Dominion and Provincial Government Securities	617,939
Railway and other Bonds and Stocks	2,880,973
Notes and Cheques of other Banks...	1,690,470
Current Loans and Discounts, and other Assets	39,160,440
Bank Premises...	600,000
	$99,332,072

THE BANK OF MONTREAL opened for business on Monday, 3rd November, 1817, in premises in a building belonging to the Armour Estate, situated on St. Paul Street, between St. Nicholas and St. Francois Xavier Streets, with a Paid-up CAPITAL of $350,000.

The first PRESIDENT was John Gray, and the first CASHIER was Robert Griffin.

In the year 1819 the CAPITAL was increased to $650,000, and in the following year to $750,000. In 1829 the capital was $850,000 ; in 1841, $2,000,000 ; in 1845, $3,000,000 ; in 1855, $4,000,000 ; in 1869, $6,000,000 ; in 1873, $12,000,000, at which it now stands.

In the first full year (1819) of the Bank's operations, a DIVIDEND was paid at the rate of 8 percent per annum, and since then (with the exception of the years 1827 and 1828, when the Bank did not pay any dividend), the annual dividends have ranged from 6 percent to 16 percent, (or say a dividend of 12 percent with a bonus of 4 percent), according to the earnings. But of late years 10 percent per annum has been the rate paid.

After 8 percent had been paid as dividend in 1819, a balance of $4,168 remained on hand, and was laid aside as a REST. From that date of small beginnings the REST has steadily grown. In

BANK OF MONTREAL—*Continued.*

1825 it was $30,780, going down to $12,064 in the following year, and then up again to $107,084 two years later; in 1830 it stood at $31,360. Five years later it stood at $50,660, reaching $197,828 in 1837; in 1840 it showed $89,480; in 1850, $120,192; in 1860, $740,000; in 1870, $3,000,000; 1880, $5,000,000; in 1883, $5,750,000; in 1884, $6,000,000; and it now stands at $7,000,000, and there are additional Undivided Profits amounting to $764,703.

On the 1st January, 1858, the MONTREAL BRANCH was established as a distinct and separate business from the Head Office, Mr. E. H. King being appointed as its first Manager.

In the year 1862, the designation of the Chief Officer of the Bank was changed from Cashier to that of General Manager. Mr. David Davidson was the first General Manager.

In 1863 the Bank of Montreal was appointed Banker in Canada for the Canadian Government, and on 1st January, 1893, Mr. E. S. Clouston being General Manager at the time, it became their Financial Agent in Great Britain also.

BRANCHES

MONTREAL (H. V. Meredith, Local Manager).—West End, 2332 St. Catherine Street; Seigneurs Street, 2532 Notre Dame; Point St. Charles, 1 Centre Street.

ONTARIO.—Almonte, Belleville, Brantford, Brockville, Chatham, Cornwall, Deseronto, Fort William, Goderich, Guelph, Hamilton, Kingston, Lindsay, London, Ottawa, Perth, Peterboro, Picton, Sarnia, Stratford, St. Mary's, Toronto (Yonge Street), Wallaceburg.

NEW BRUNSWICK—Chatham, Fredericton, Moncton, St. John.

NOVA SCOTIA.—Amherst, Halifax, Sydney,

MANITOBA AND N. W. T.—Winnipeg, Calgary, Lethbridge, Regina.

BRITISH COLUMBIA.—Greenwood, Nelson, New Denver, New Westminster, Rossland, Vancouver, Vernon, Victoria.

NEWFOUNDLAND.—St. John's.

GREAT BRITAIN.—Abchurch Lane, E. C. London, Alexander Lang. Manager.

UNITED STATES.—New York, 59 Wall Street, R. G. Hebden and J. M. Greta, Agents; Chicago, Cor. La Salle and Monroe Streets, J. W. De C. O'Grady, Manager.

SAVINGS BANK DEPARTMENTS connected with each Canadian Branch, and Deposits received and interest allowed at current rates.

COLLECTIONS at all points in the Dominion of Canada and the United States undertaken at most favorable rates.

TRAVELLERS' LETTERS OF CREDIT issued, negotiable in all parts of the world.

TARIFF FOR HACKNEY CARRIAGES.

ONE HORSE VEHICLES.—One or two persons, 15 minutes, 25 cents; 30 minutes, 40 cents; the first hour 75 cents, and 60 cents for every subsequent hour. Three or four persons, 40 cents for 15 minutes, 60 cents for 30 minutes, $1.00 for the first hour and 75 cents for every subsequent hour.

TWO HORSE VEHICLES.—One or two persons, 50 cents for 15 minutes, 65 cents for 30 minutes, and $1.00 per hour. For three or four persons, 65 cents for 15 minutes, 75 cents for 30 minutes and $1.25 per hour.

UNITED STATES CUSTOMS.
(Baggage Examination.)

Travellers are permitted to take with them as baggage across the line, free of duty :—Souvenirs, in the shape of Views, Indian Curiosities, etc., on which the duty would not exceed $2.00. Goods amounting to over $2.00 of duty charges are liable to duty for the full amount. The duty on Lithographic Views is 25 percent; Photographs, 20; Indian Curiosities according to value of texture. Furs, 30 percent.

(The word Tariff is derived from the town of Tariffa, on the coast of Spain, near the entrance to the Straits of Gibraltar, where customs were originally levied of ships trading in the Mediterranean Sea.)

Postal Rates.

LETTERS.—Canada and U.S., 2c. per 1 oz.; Great Britain, Newfoundland, and all other British Colonies, 2c. per ½ oz.; all other countries, 5c. per ½ oz.

NEWSPAPERS are sent free from office of publication to any place other than place of publication, in Canada, Newfoundland and U.S. Newspapers otherwise posted, 1 cent per 4 oz. Great Britain, 1 cent per 2 oz.

BOOK POST.—Canada, 1 cent per 4 oz.; U.S., Newfoundland and Great Britain, 1 cent per 2 oz.

REGISTRATION—Letters, Books, etc., 5 cents in all cases.

PARCEL POST, for Canada only, 6 cents per 4 oz. Parcels must not exceed 5 lbs.

PATTERN AND SAMPLE POST—Not to exceed 24 oz., 1 cent per 4 oz. U.S., special rate per parcel 10 cents. To U.S. not to exceed 8 oz.

MONEY ORDERS may be had either from the Post-Office, Dominion or Canadian Express, or any of the banks.

Street letter boxes in Montreal are visited four times daily, viz.: 9.15 a.m., 12.30 p.m., 5.30 p.m., and 7.45 p.m.

MURRAY'S
ILLUSTRATED GUIDE

TO

MONTREAL AND VICINITY

CONTAINING

MAP OF MONTREAL, DESCRIPTION OF PLACES OF INTEREST,
CAB TARIFF, POSTAGE RATES, STREET DIRECTORY, ETC.
WITH GENERAL CANADIAN REFERENCE TABLES.

COMPLIED FROM THE MOST AUTHENTIC SOURCES BY

NORMAN MURRAY.

DIEU ET MON DROIT

EIGHTH EDITION.   FIFTEENTH THOUSAND.

MONTREAL :
NORMAN MURRAY, PUBLISHER.

NEW YORK LIFE BUILDING.   Montreal

MONTREAL PAST AND PRESENT.

"The wolf also shall dwell with the lamb, and the leopard shall lie
down with the kid ; and the calf and the young lion and the fatling
together ; and a little child shall lead them."—Isaiah.

Rose-wreath and fleur-de-ly's
Shamrock and thistle be
Joined to the maple tree
Now and for aye.

—*John Reade.*

The City of Montreal, the commercial metropolis of the
Dominion of Canada, is built on an island of the same name formed
by the River Ottawa debouching into the River St. Lawrence, at its
western and eastern extremities, the former near St. Ann's, 21 miles
from Montreal, the latter at Bout de l'Ile. This island is triangular
in shape, and is about thirty miles long and ten broad, situated in
latitude 45° 31' North, and Longitude 78° 35' West, and 250 miles
above salt water.

Montreal was founded on the 8th of May, 1642, by Maisonneuve.
107 years after the visit of Jacques Cartier and his crew in 1535.
Jacques Cartier was the first European who visited the locality. On
the arrival of Jacques Cartier there was an Indian village called
Hochelaga on the site of the Montreal of to-day. The village was
situated where the English Cathedral, at the Corner of University
and St. Catarine Streets, now stands. What is now known as
Hochelaga was for many years a French town, two miles east of
Montreal, but is now joined to the City of Montreal.

On the 2nd day of October, 1535, Jacques Cartier landed at Hochelaga. Being conducted through the town by the friendly Indians
they next guided him to the top of the Mountain, and he was so
struck with the beauty of the situation that he named the mountain
"Mount Royal."

Our local historian, Mr. Lighthall, Mayor of Westmount, following the example of the author of Knickerbocker's History of New
York, goes back some hundred million years ago, when the site of
our Metropolis was in the bottom of a gulf, then he traces up the
development of the elevation of the crust through the formation of
subterranean fires and finally the levelling off of the top of the
mountain by a huge iceberg.   If he could only tell us where the
"iceberg" dropped off the broken pieces we would be still more
indebted to him.   The space at our disposal for this edition will
not permit us to go farther back than Jacques Cartier's visit, and
quote his description of the Montreal of that day, nearly five hundred years ago. The population then was about 1,500 people. After
relating the hospitable reception he received and the exchange of
presents, he proceeds as follows :—"The lands were tilled in large
fields of corn.   In the midst of those fields is situated the said town
of Hochelaga, near and adjoining the mountain. . . . . The said
town is quite round, and palisaded with wood in three rows, in the
form of a pyramid, interlaced above, having the middle row in
perpendicular, then lined with wood laid along, well joined and
corded in a style of their own, and is of the height of about two
lances.   There is in the town but one gate and entrance, which
shuts with bars, on which, and in several places on said palisade, is
a kind of gallery, with ladders to mount them which are furnished
with rocks and stones for the guard and defence thereof.   There are
in that town about fifty houses, each at most about fifty paces long
and twelve or fifteen paces wide, all made of wood, covered and
furnished in great pieces of bark as large as tables, well sewed
artificially after their manner ; and in them are several halls and
chambers, and in the middle of said houses is a great hall on the
ground, where they make their fires and live in common ; then they
retire to their said chambers, the men with their wives and children.
And likewise they have granaries above their houses where they
put their corn, whereof they make their bread which they call
"Caracom."

Champlain visited the place in 1611—76 years after Jacques
Cartier's visit, and founded a trading post on the site of the old
Custom House Square—renamed a few years ago " La Place Royale."

There are several legends and traditions about old Hochelaga
and the misfortune of its original inhabitants.

At the time of Jacques Cartier's visit the town was flourishing, and the surrounding district was covered with corn fields. One story is to the effect that a Senaca Chief prohibited his son from marrying a certain maid of his own tribe. The maid got into a passion and vowed that she should marry no one except one that would kill the chief who interfered with her happiness. A young Huron filled the conditions, and obtained his bride, but the whole of the two tribes took part afterwards in the quarrel with disastrous results to the once prosperous and happy citizens of Hochelaga.

The following very interesting legend and prophecy was at one time very common amongst the Mohawk Indians, though now barely remembered :—

Long, long ago there was a great lake where the Island of Montreal now stands, and the Mohawks dwelt upon its borders and were happy. Then bad people came and drove the Indians into the water, killing many of them ; and the Great Spirit when he saw the Mohawks so badly treated, raised up a country for them out of the lake and stocked it with game and fruits and maize, and gave it to the Mohawks; but there was no mountain. Then the bad people came over to the Island and took possession of it, and drove the Mohawks away to the Isle of Jesus, which they made their hunting ground. Then when they stood on the shore one evening they saw a great fire leap up on the island, and there were dreadful peals of thunder, and terrible flashes of lightning, and all the bad people were killed; and after a while, when the smoke had cleared away, the Mohawks saw the Mountain, and they went back and took possession of the Island, where they lived happily until attacked by the Algonquins and Wyandots. Then the white man came and drove all the Indians away. This is the legend. There is also a prophecy that one day the Mohawks shall see the fire break out in the Mountain again, and that the whole Island of Montreal will sink, and the great lake again spread over the spot where the island now stands. The legends and the prophecy are pretty, and geological research may show some foundation for the upheaval.

The first clearing for the city was made where the Custom House now stands. The city proper is about four and a half miles long by two broad, and over 200 miles of streets and lanes. Montreal is 315 miles nearer to Liverpool than the city of New York, and one-third of the whole distance, by way of the St. Lawrence, is in com-

paratively smooth water.   The distance from Montreal to Chicago
by the St. Lawrence system is 185 miles less than the distance from
New York to the same city.   Montreal is 334 miles from Boston,
400 miles from New York, 845 miles from Chicago, and 2,750 miles
from Liverpool.

British troops were stationed at Montreal till 1870.   The Barracks
were situated where the C. P. R. Dalhousie Station now stands.
The Military cemetery and powder magazine and store-rooms were
on St. Helen's Island.

Montreal surrendered to the British forces under Generals
Murray and Amherst on the 8th September, 1760, a year after the
capture of Quebec.   It was taken by the Americans on the 12th of
November, 1775, and retaken by the British on the 15th of June,
1776.   The English-speaking portion of the population were so dis-
gusted with the Rebellion Losses Bill passed by the Liberals in 1847,
that, when the Governor-General, Lord Elgin, entered the Parliament House (erected where the St. Ann's Market now stands) on
the 25th of April to give his assent to the measure, they gathered
together from all quarters of the city, and entering the Parliament
House they drove out the members and set fire to the building.
That was the last Parliament held in Montreal.

The census figures were not published as we go to press, but it
is estimated that the population of the city and suburbs is at least
300,000.

The population of Montreal proper (Government census of 1891)
was 216,650, or 245,971, including St. Henri, Ste. Cunegonde, Cote St.
Antoine and Mile End.   This is over 25 percent increase during the
last decade.   Over one-half of the population are of French, one-
fifth of Irish, one-seventh of English and one-seventeenth of Scotch
origin (but the one-seventeenth of Scotch origin have as large a
share in the enterprise and business of Montreal as any of the other
nationalities which form one-half, one-fifth, or one-seventh of the
population), and as to religion, about two-thirds are Roman Catholics.   The general good feeling existing between parties of different
shades of opinion renders Montreal less subject to party disturban-
ces than other cities of the same population.   This rule, of course,
like every other rule, had one or two exceptions ; but the following
two instances show that the above rule has been very well followed.
In the olden times, just after the Conquest, the Protestants used one

of the Roman Catholic churches after morning mass. For 20 years after 1766, the Church of England people occupied the Church of the Recollets every Sunday afternoon. The Presbyterians used the same church before 1792, and when the congregation moved to their first church in St. Gabriel Street, they presented to the priests of the Recollet Church a gift of candles for the high altar, and of wine for the mass, as a token of good-will, and thanks for the gratuitous use of the church.

The Bonsecours Church was very nigh being swept away a few years ago to make room for a railway station, but some Protestants, actuated by a love of the picturesque, and out of regard for the memory of the good Sister by whom it was founded, made such a noise about it that the Bishop interefered to prevent the sale.

Louis Joseph Papineau, who, with William Lyon Mackenzie, took the lead in the troubles of 1837-38, had his headquarters in Montreal.

It may be as well to remark here that these two men, Mackenzie and Papineau, did more for the cause of freedom than any other two men that ever lived in Canada. Like many other good men they were not sufficiently honored till they were gone. It is now admitted by all parties that there was much room for reform in the government of the day.

On the 9th of June, 1853, Father Gavazzi, a celebrated lecturer, formerly a famous Roman Catholic priest, lectured against the Church of Rome in Zion Congregational Church (now Small's Clothing House), and a riot ensued, in which about 40 persons were either killed or wounded.

One of the most unfortunate events in the history of Montreal was the murder of Thomas Hackett, an Orangeman, on the 12th of July, 1877, by a gang of Fenians, on Victoria Square, near the Queen's monument. Several of the bullet shot marks may yet be seen in the stone wall at 15 Victoria Square, opposite the Queen's monument.

The second steamer built on the continent of America was built at Montreal, by Mr. John Molson, and was called the " Accommodation." She made her first voyage in 36 hours between Montreal and Quebec, on the 3rd and 4th November, 1809.

From 1685 to 1801 Montreal was surrounded by a wall, extending along the site of Fortification Lane from Victoria Square to Dalhousie Square, at the Canadian Pacific Railway Depot. From

Victoria Square the walls extended down to the river, about the site of McGill Street. The city then was of triangular shape, the small angle pointing towards the east.

Montreal is less subject to epidemics than many other cities of the same size, although the smallpox got hold of it in 1885, on account of the vast majority of the French-Canadians being prejudiced against vaccination. The number of deaths was 3,164 ; of these, 2,887 were French-Canadians, 181 other Catholics, and 96 Protestants.

The first steamer to cross the Atlantic, "The Royal William," had her engines built in Montreal by Mr. John Bennett, in 1831. The hull was built at Quebec by Mr. James Goudie. She made the trip across the Atlantic in 1833. The "Royal William," was the first war vessel propelled by steam. She was bought by the Spanish Government and her name changed to "Isabella Secunda."

NOTES RECEIVED FROM MR. LAMBE, OF THE INLAND REVENUE.

Part of the old fortification wall may still be seen between Notre Dame and St. James Street (232) near Dollard Lane.

There is an old gate in the cellar of Henderson's Fur Store, on St. James Street, that led through the wall. The old town well was on the site of Maisonneuve's Monument. Part of the old wall was built of flat and part of round stones.

Old ruins of Baron de Longueuil's house may still be seen on St. Helen's Island, at the back of the restaurant.

Slavery was abolished in Canada in 1792, and the Jews were emancipated in 1830.

CHRONOLOGY OF MONTREAL.

1525—October 2, Jacques Cartier visits Hochelaga (Montreal).

1611—Champlain visits the Island—76 years after Jacques Cartier.

1642—May 18, Montreal founded by Maisonneuve.

1644—March 3, the Battle of Champ de Mars (see Historical Tablets No. 13, page 46.)

1685—The fortification wall was built around Montreal.

1760—Montreal surrenders to the British forces under Generals Murray and Amherst.

1765—There were only 136 Protestants in Montreal, and 500 in Canada, (not including the army).

1775—May 1, a bust of George III. is found in Montreal, adorned with beads and mitre and the words " Pope of Canada and Sot of England."   A reward of 500 guineas was offered for the apprehension of the culprit, but without avail.

1775—September 25, Ethan Allan and his fellow Yankee invaders captured at Longue Point.

1775—November 12, Montreal taken by the Americans.

1776—June 12, General Montgomery (U. S.) invades Montreal.

1776—June 16, Arnold's (U. S.) army retreats from Montreal and Montreal is again under the British flag.

1792—St. Gabriel Street Presbyterian Church—the first Protestant church in Montreal built.

1801—The old fortification walls were pulled down.

1809—August 17, foundation stone of Nelson's Monument, Jacques Cartier Square, laid.

1809—November 3, John Molson's steamboat " Accommodation " starts from Montreal for Quebec.

1817—Bank of Montreal, the first bank in Canada, opened.

1821—July 17, work commenced on the Lachine canal.

1822—Montreal General Hospital finished.

1822—This year the population of Montreal was only 18,767.

1825—Lachine canal finished.

1826—McGill College founded.

1829—Notre Dame Church opened.

1844—L'Institut Canadien founded.

1847—Montreal Parliament Buildings burned by a Tory mob.

1847—6,000 immigrants (mostly Irish) die of ship fever.

1848—Jesuits' College opened.

1852—July 8, great fire in Montreal ; 11,000 houses burned.

1853—June 9, Gavazzi Riots.

1856—December 10. Christ Church Cathedral burned.

1861—First street railway in Montreal.

1868—The foundation of St. Peter's (St. James) Cathedral laid.

1875—September 2, Guibord Riots.   R.C. mob prevent the burial of Joseph Guibord, a French-Canadian R.C. and member of L'Institut Canadien, from being buried in his own lot in Cote des Neiges cemetery.

1575—November 16 : Following judgment of Privy Council, Guibord is buried, being accompanied to the cemetery by a strong military detachment.   His grave is one of the sights of the R.C. cemetery.   It is near the entrance, and is easily distinguished by the large rock placed on top of it.

1577—July 12, Murder of Hacket.

1879—July 31, Consolidated Bank fails.

1885—Smallpox kills 3,164 people, mostly French-Canadians.

HOTELS.

The principal Hotels are :—Windsor Hotel, Dominion Square ; St. Lawrence Hall, St. James Street , near the Post-Office; Queen's Hotel; Balmoral Hotel; Albion Hotel; Savoy, on Victoria Street; St. James Hotel, and Turkish Bath Hotel.

CHURCHES.

After the stranger has fixed on a hotel to stop in, the first point of attraction in Montreal is the churches.   Montreal is noted for the number of churches it contains, as well as for the number of its charitable institutions.   There are at present 97 churches in Montreal and suburbs, or one for every 2,800 people.   Of these 20 are Roman Catholic, 24 Presbyterian, 20 Episcopal, 1 Reformed Episcopal, 12 Methodist, 5 Congregational, 7 Baptist, 1 Swedenborgian or New Jerusalem Church, 1 Unitarian, and 4 Jewish Synagogues, 1 German Lutheran, 1 Christian Scientist, 1 Advent Christian, 1 Catholic Apostolic.   There are seven Protestant churches in which the services are conducted in the French language.

Mark Twain remarked at the Windsor once that he never saw so many churches within a stone's throw of each other before.

St. Peter's Cathedral, properly speaking the Cathedral of St. James (he being its patron saint), now in course of construction on Dominion Square, demands first attention.   It is being built after the model of St. Peter's at Rome, of which, generally speaking, it is about half the dimensions.   The foundation of it was laid in 1868. The dimensions of St. Peter's at Rome are : length, 615 feet ; breadth, 286 feet; and height, 435 to the top of the dome.

The following are the dimensions of St. Peter's of Montreal, copied from the figures on the plan of the cathedral, very kindly

given to the compiler of this little book, by a gentleman in actual
charge of the construction.   The exact height to the top of the
cross is 258 feet, that is, 240 feet to the top of the dome, and the
cross being 18 feet high, makes the entire height 258 feet.   The
breadth of the cross is 12 feet.   It weighs 1,500 lbs.   The stone work
is 132 feet high.   Above this is the dome, 108 feet of wood work,
with the cross 18 feet high, fixed on the top.   The extreme length
of the building is 333 feet exterior and 295 feet interior.   The
greatest breadth is 222 feet exterior and 216 interior.   The general
breadth is 150 feet.   The general thickness of the wall is between
three and four feet.   The foundation wall is eight feet thick and
eight feet deep below the surface.   The circumference of the outside of the dome is 240 feet.   The view of the city from the dome
excels by far every other view in the city.

The parish church of Notre Dame, erroneously called the French
Cathedral, stands upon Place d'Armes, Notre Dame Street, (the
coldest spot in Montreal at all seasons of the year).   It is built after
the model of Notre Dame (Our Lady) in Paris.   It holds 10,000
people comfortably, and when crowded, as it often is, it has been
known to hold 15,000 people.   The length of the church is 255 feet,
and the breadth 134 feet.   The two principal towers are 227 feet
high.   The Bourdon bell, the largest in America, weighs 24,780 lbs.,
and cost $25,000.   It is 8 feet 7 inches in diameter, and 6 feet 9
inches high.   It is 1 foot thick.   Clappers weigh 860 lbs.   Besides
this enormous bell there are 10 other bells, which, when rung on
great occasions, make very agreeable chimes.   It is stated that the
entire church cost over $6,000,000.   It is the largest ecclesiastical
edifice in America, except the Cathedral of Mexico.   It has 19
double confession boxes, where 19 priests can hear 38 confessions at
one time.   It has two galleries, one above the other.   The corner
stone was laid in 1824, and the first mass performed in 1829.

The Church of Notre Dame de Lourdes, built in 1874, for the
purpose of illustrating the doctrine of the Immaculate Conception, is
the most beautiful in the city.   The adoration of the Virgin under
this name dates from the 11th February, 1858, when it is stated that
the Blessed Virgin appeared to a young Shepherdess fourteen years
of age, named Bernadette Soubirous, at the Grotto of Massabielle, on
the banks of the river Gave, near the town of Lourdes (Loord), in
the diocese of Tarbes, in the upper Pyrenees, in the south-west of

France, 530 miles from Paris. It is stated that the Blessed Virgin appeared to this girl eighteen times, and told her that "she was the Immaculate Conception," and sent a message by her to the clergy to tell them to build a chapel for her on that rock. It is also further stated that she revealed a secret to her, which she told her not to make known. It is also further stated that water, with healing qualities, gushed out of the rock at that time, and continued to flow ever since. In the basement of Notre Dame de Lourdes, at Montreal, is a fac-simile of the Grotto at Lourdes, which strangers interested in such things should not fail to visit. Lourdes is noted for its excellent chocolate, and is in the neighborhood of the best mineral springs of the Pyrenees.—(Anna T. Sadlier's, Wonders of Lourdes.)   N.B.—Is it the mineral qualities of the water or the religious nature of the place that effects the cure?

The Church of Notre Dame de Bonsecours (Our Lady of Good Help) is the oldest church in the city, being erected in 1771.   There is a grand statue of the Virgin erected on this church with an elevator to go up to it.   It was originally intended to erect this statue on Mount Royal, but the citizens were not unanimous about the choice, so it was decided to erect it where there would be no opposition.

Of the other Roman Catholic Churches the most interesting to tourists and others are: the Jesuits' Church, on Bleury Street ; St. Patrick's Church, on St. Alexander Street ; Notre Dame de Nazareth, and the Church of St. James.

PROTESTANT CHURCHES.

Christ Church Cathedral (Episcopal), on St. Catharine Street, is said to be the finest specimen of gothic architecture in North America.   St. George's Church, and the Church of St. James the Apostle are the next in importance of the Episcopal Churches in point of architecture.   St. George's (Low Church), has the largest Protestant congregation in Montreal.   The Methodists can now boast of having one of the grandest churches in Montreal in St. James Church, St. Catherine Street.

Of the Presbyterian churches, Crescent Street Church, St. Paul's Church, and the American Presbyterian Church receive the most attention for architecture.   St. Gabriel Street Presbyterian Church is the oldest existing Protestant church in Canada.   It was erected in 1792.

THE CHURCH OF THE MESSIAH.

CHRISTIAN UNITARIAN.

This Church stands in part upon an interesting site. A tablet upon its wall has the following inscription :  " Here stood Beaver Hall, built 1800, burned 1848 ; Mansion of Joseph Frobisher, one of the founders of the North-West Company, which made Montreal for years the fur trading centre of America." The church was opened for worship in 1858. It was much damaged by fire in 1869 and then renewed. An earlier building on the same sight was dedicated to Unitarian services in 1845. Previously, the congregation, which was organized in 1842, had worshipped in the little building (recently demolished) which stood on the corner of Fortification Lane and Victoria (then Hay Market) Square. Its first pastor was the late Rev. John Cordner, LL.D., the Rev. E. F. Hayward and the Rev. J. B. Green were each for a time associated with him. The present minister is the Rev. William S. Barnes.

The Young Men's Christian Association, the oldest institution of the kind on the continent, on Dominion Square. Reading Room and Library, open from 8 a.m. to 10 p.m. Young men looking for employment, whether resident in Montreal or not, would do well to call. Young men's prayer meeting, Saturday, from 8 to 9 p.m. Sunday services :—Men's Bible Class, 9.30 to 10.30 a.m., 3 to 4 p.m.

The Sailors' Institute, on Commissioners Street, is a kindred institution to the Y.M.C.A. There is also the Young Women's Christian Association Rooms. A very useful institution.

VICTORIA BRIDGE.

Victoria Bridge, the longest bridge in the world at the time of its erection, was considered the eighth wonder of the world. It is one and seven-eighths miles long between stonework, and two miles long including stone work approaches. It is made of twenty-five tubes, supported by twenty-four piers, and two end butments. The lower side of the centre tube is sixty feet above the summer level of the River St. Lawrence. It was erected in 1859 by James Hodges, from the designs of Robert Stephenson and Alexander M. Ross.

It was formally opened by the Prince of Wales in 1860. The height from the bed of the river to the top of the centre tube is 108 feet. The greatest depth of water during the summer season is about 22 feet, but in the spring the water sometimes rises over 20 feet above the summer level of the river. In the spring of 1886 the water rose 25 feet above the average summer level. The centre has an elevation of about 20 feet above the ends. The current at the bridge runs at the rate of seven miles an hour. The bridge cost over $6,000,000. It belongs to the Grand Trunk Railway Company. Trains generally take from four and a half to five minutes to cross the bridge. It took five and one-half years to build it.

THE LACHINE CANAL is eight and a quarter miles long, and over-comes a total rise of 45 feet. It has five locks, 270 feet long and 45 feet wide. Vessels drawing 12 feet of water can pass through it. The width of the canal varies from 163 to 208 feet. The first ground was broken at Lachine on the 17th of July, 1821.

WATER WORKS.—The water of the city is taken from the River St. Lawrence, about a mile above the Lachine Rapids, at a point 37 feet above the summer level of the harbor of Montreal. One branch of the aqueduct starts at that point, and another branch starts from a point a little over half a mile above. Both unite and form a canal about five miles long, to the wheel house, at the west end of the city. From the wheel house the water is pumped to the large reservoir, on the side of the mountain, a distance of about three miles. The large reservoir, dug out of the solid rock, is 200 feet above the level of the St. Lawrence. It is 810 feet long, by 377 feet wide, and 24 feet deep. It has a capacity of 36½ millions of gallons. From the large reservoir the water that supplies the city above Sherbrooke Street is pumped to a smaller reservoir 70 yards

further up, on the side of the mountain. The water works of the
city cost $6,000,000.

THE LACHINE RAPIDS are about seven miles above Montreal,
and about two miles below the town of Lachine. The Rapids extend
about half a mile in length between Heron Island on the north and
Devil's Island on the south. During the summer season trains leave
Bonaventure Depot 7.55 a.m. and 5 p.m., to connect with the boats
shooting the Rapids in the morning and evening. The round trip
may be made in about two hours—return tickets 50c. Opposite
Lachine is the Indian village of Caughnawaga, where a remnant of
the Mohawk tribe of Iroquois are settled upon a reserve. These
Indians are famous for their skill in boating, so that when the British Government, in 1884, sent a boat expedition up the cataracts of
the Nile, for the relief of Khartoum, a gang of fifty Caughnawagas
were sent to lead the expedition, and how satisfactorily they performed their task is known to all who took an interest in the
history of these times.

PARKS AND SQUARES.

Mount Royal, so called by Jacques Cartier on his first visit to
Canada, 1535, in honor of the King of France, rises over 700 feet
above the level of the River St. Lawrence. The mountain peak
covers 430 acres of ground. A fine view of the city and surrounding country may be got from the summit. Looking southward
across the river, the first mountain to the left is Montarville ; seven
pretty lakes are concealed in the recesses of the mountain. Next is
Beloeil mountain (or St. Hilaire), with the ruin of a chapel on the
summit. A depression in the midst of the mountain is occupied by
a lake of singular clearness and depth. Next is Rougemont, almost
concealing the Yamaska mountain behind it ; and to the right the
conical shape of Mount Johnson, or Monoir, sharply breaks above
the level surface. In the far distance are to be seen the Green
Mountains of Vermont to the left, and the Adirondacks, in New
York to the right.

The cemeteries may be mentioned in connection with Mount
Royal Park, of which they now form a part. The first Catholic
cemetery was situated at Place d'Armes, and the Protestant cemetery was located where St. James and St. Peter Streets meet. As

the city extended the Roman Catholic cemetery was removed to Dominion Square, and the Protestant cemetery to Dufferin Square, on Dorchester Street east.   There was also a civil and military cemetery on Papineau road and on St. Helen's Island; and, finally, they were all removed to their present location.   In the Roman Catholic cemetery the ascent to Mount Calvary, by the 14 stations of the cross, appeals to the devotion of Roman Catholics, and interests Protestants, as being a feature not met with in the cemeteries usually visited.

ST. HELEN'S ISLAND, now used as a public park, is the most popular place for picnics in the city.   The island is named after Hélène Boullé, Champlain's wife, the first European lady that came to Canada.   It was used for many years by the British Government as a depot for military stores and a station for troops.   The fort and barracks still remain.

Viger Square, or as it is popularly called, Viger Garden, on St. Denis Street.

THE CHAMP-DE-MARS, upon Craig Street, is a fine exercise ground for troops.

JACQUES CARTIER SQUARE, near the City Hall and Court House, has a fine outlook upon the river.   A column, surmounted by a statue of Lord Nelson, is placed at the head of the square.   It was erected in 1808, by the merchants of Montreal, shortly after the death of the Admiral at Trafalgar.

VICTORIA SQUARE, at the junction of St. James and McGill Streets, is on the site of the old hay market.   The name was changed in 1860, in honor of the Queen, on the occasion of the visit of the Prince of Wales to Canada.   Upon it is a colossal statue of the Queen, in bronze, by Marshall Wood, an English artist.

DOMINION SQUARE is the finest square in the city as to site.   Till late years it was known as the Catholic Cemetery.   The Windsor Hotel, St. Peter's Cathedral, and several other churches, give it importance architecturally.   (See list of streets, etc.)

PLACE D'ARMES (so called on account of the battle that was once fought here with the Indians), the site of the first Roman Catholic cemetery in Montreal, is opposite Notre Dame Church; it is surrounded on all sides by important buildings.   This is said to be the coolest spot in Montreal at all seasons of the year.

THE ST. LAWRENCE.

THE RIVER ST. LAWRENCE is 2,200 miles long. Its remotest source is the St. Louis, a small stream falling into the upper end of Lake Superior. It is the fourteenth longest river in the world, and the fifth longest river in America. From Quebec to Montreal a short distance below Quebec to the Gulf of St. Lawrence, it varies from 10 to 35 miles in width. Half-way between Montreal and Quebec it widens out into Lake St. Peter, which is 20 miles long and 9 wide. Jacques Cartier sailed for the first time on the Gulf of St. Lawrence on the 10th of August, 1535, and that being St. Lawrence Day, he named that body of water in honor of the saint, and the Gulf and River St. Lawrence have been known by that name ever since.

At Quebec the river rises 15 feet, but it ceases to be observed at the lower end of Lake St. Peter. The depth of the river is so great that Quebec was one of the few ports in America which the "Great Eastern" was able to visit.

PUBLIC BUILDINGS.

The principal public buildings are :—The Court House, Bonsecours Market (should be visited on Tuesday or Friday), the Custom House, the Examining Warehouse, the new City Hall, the Harbor Commissioners' Building, Inland Revenue Office, the office of the Board of Arts and Agriculture, and the Exhibition Buildings and Grounds, Mile End.

RAILWAY STATIONS.

Montreal has three of the best railway stations on the continent, all new. The Grand Trunk and Canadian Pacific Railways have Bonaventure and Windsor Stations in the West end of the city, and the Canadian Pacific Railway has also Dalhousie Station in the east end for the Quebec line. The Grand Trunk Railway depot at Bonaventure, or St. James Street, and the Canadian Pacific Railway Station, on Windsor Street, should be visited by any one who has time.

NEW YORK LIFE BUILDING.

One of the most substantial and valuable buildings in the whole Dominion is the chief office of the New York Life Insurance Company, which was erected some few years since at the corner of Place d'Armes and St. James Street, to be the home of their Cana-

dian business. After providing for the requirements of the
Company, there is a large portion of the Building which is sub-let
to tenants. It is a hive of industry during the busy business hours,
and its three elevators are kept constantly at work, and an average
of 12,000 or 13,000 persons per week make use of them.

The Company commenced business as far back as 1841, and
entered Canada in 1883. While their Building is an ornament,
they would probably consider that their enterprise has been repaid,
because last year they paid for over five and a quarter millions of
new business in the Dominion of Canada, which is a larger amount
than has ever been done by any other company, Canadian, British
or foreign.

It is not unusual for visitors to Montreal to go up the tower of
this building, from which they can get an excellent view of the
whole city, the attendants are courteous, and there is no charge.

The building is eight stories above the ground, but in addition
there are two stories below the pavement, one rented for offices, and
the lower one used for the machinery and electric plant which
works the electric light and the elevators.

Among other important offices in the Building there are those
occupied by the Quebec Bank, as well as the Office of the Montreal
Gas Company. A great many of the tenants belong to the legal
profession, there being a law library in the Building provided by
the Company for the use of tenants, which is one of the most valuable in Canada.

A USEFUL LIFE.

There is no more useful calling in our day and generation than that
of the druggist and chemist. The successful druggist requires a high
order of intelligence and a close attention to business. He is at
his post early and late, and he gets few holidays. Of all the many
druggists in Montreal no one has had a more honored career than
Mr. Henry R. Gray, 122 St. Lawrence Street. He is a native of
Lincolnshire, England, and came to Canada in 1858, after having
served his apprenticeship and otherwise qualifying himself for his
profession in the world's metropolis (London). With one exception, he has been engaged in the sale of drugs and medicines longer
than any other pharmacist in Montreal. It is a chronic complaint with

the Montreal public that the best men have a reluctance to enter public life. In this respect, like many others, Mr. Gray has shown a good example. His efforts for the improvement of the sanitary arrangements of this city and province are well known. He is now a member of the Provincial Board of Health, and also a member of the Council of Public Instruction. He was alderman and chairman of the local Board of Health during the fearful smallpox epidemic of 1885-6. He has made several useful discoveries in medicine. Besides those that he sold to some of the large wholesale establishments (which I am not going to advertise gratis) he has several specialties of which he has reserved the right, such as "Saponaceous Dentifrice," for the teeth, which sells for 25c a bottle, "Dental Pearline," and "Castor Fluid." Mr. Gray saves the people of his district a good deal in doctor's fees, as he often gives advice gratis which would cost his customers many dollars. One instance which came under my own observation will be sufficient without enlarging on the subject, and as he will not see this till it is printed and cannot recall it unless he buys this edition of 2,000 copies, I will relate it. A certain party (never mind who it was) asked for something. "Yes, he had it, but it cost 50c and he had something for 25c just as good."

BENEVOLENT INSTITUTIONS.

Montreal is as remarkable for the number and variety of its philanthropic institutions as it is for the number of its churches. Every national society has its "home" for those of its own nationality. The St. George's Society for English, St. Andrew's for Scotch, St. Patrick's for the Catholic Irish, and the Irish Benevolent Society for Protestant Irish, the German Society for Germans, and St. John the Baptist's for French-Canadians. The social organization of Montreal is so composite, that in order to work well many institutions require to be triplicate at best. Race and language divide the French from the English and Irish, and religion divides the English from the French and Irish; and the Irish are sub-divided by religion, so that they require two separate national benevolent societies.

The following are the principal institutions :—

BOYS' HOME.

The Boys' Home was first started in Barre Street. The first building on the present site at 117 Mountain Street was built in 1871, Mr. Charles Alexander paying for building it, the lot having been bought by some other philanthropic gentleman. The first building has been considerably enlarged since. Mr. Alexander has been president for over thirty years. Mr. J. R. Dick has been superintendent for about twenty years. Of late years he has been assisted by Mr. Gawne. In one of his annual reports the Superintendent says, "What would we ever do without Mr. Gawne?"

Royal Victoria Hospital.—This noble institution was founded in 1887 by two noble Caledonians, Lord Strathcona and Mount Royal (then Sir Donald A. Smith), and Lord Mount Stephen. It was opened in 1894. It has 215 beds with a daily average of 187 patients. Two thousand six hundred and nineteen patients were admitted during last year. The most radical reformer cannot object to such use of wealth.

Protestant Insane Asylum, Verdun.

The Montreal General Hospital, corner Dorchester and St. Dominique, founded in 1822.

Protestant House of Industry and Refuge, 680 Dorchester Street.

The Mackay Institute, for Protestant Deaf Mutes, Cote St. Luc Road.

The Montreal Dispensary, 145 St. Antoine Street.

The Ladies' Benevolent Institution, 31 Berthelet Street.

The Andrew's Home, in connection with the Episcopal churches, in Palace Street.

Protestant Infants' Home, 508 Guy Street.

St. Margaret's Nursery for Foundlings and House of Mercy for Fallen Women (Episcopalian), 12 Kensington Ave., Cote St. Antoine.

St. Margaret's Home, Church of England, 660 Sherbrooke Street.

Home for Friendless Women, 418 St. Antoine Street.

Protestant Orphan Asylum, 2409 St. Catharine Street.

St. Andrews Home, 403 Aqueduct Street.

St. George's Home, 139 St. Antoine Street.

The Hervey Institute, Mountain Street, near Dorchester.

The Montreal Maternity, 93 St. Urbain St.

The Western Hospital, 1251 Dorchester Street.

The Women's Protective Immigration Society, 141 Mansfield Street.

Society for the Prevention of Cruelty to Animals, 189 St. James Street.

Grey Nunnery, corner of Guy and Dorchester Streets. At one time this institution served as a hospital. It is now more of a foundling institution and boarding-house for old men and old women. The name "Grey Nuns" was first given them in derision. (See Appleton's Canadian Guide Book). The peculiar dress worn by the sisterhood of that order was adopted by them for the first time in August, 1775; seventeen years after the foundation of the order. The order was founded in 1738, the first list of members being Mme. d'Youville, with three pious companions and four or five infirm poor. In the year 1747, the management of the General Hospital of Ville-Marie, founded in 1694, was given to the sisters of this order. During the year of the ship fever in 1847-8, these sisters took a leading part in their attendance on suffering humanity at that time. This institution has about 890 inmates, between nuns and patients. Although visitors are always welcome, twelve o'clock noon is the time that is best for visitors to call, as special preparations for the reception of visitors are made then.

On a little spot of ground (neatly fenced in) at Point St. Charles, near the end of Victoria Bridge, is an enormous stone, called the Immigrants' Memorial Stone, taken from the bed of the River St. Lawrence, and erected on a column of stone work by the workingmen employed in the construction of the Victoria Bridge, bearing the following inscription : — "To preserve from desecration the remains of 6,000 immigrants, who died of ship fever, A.D. 1847-8, this stone is erected by the workingmen of Messrs. Peto, Brasseys and Betts, employed in the construction of the Victoria Bridge, A.D. 1859." (This stone has been removed.)

The Hotel Dieu Hospital is the oldest institution of the kind in Montreal, being founded in 1644, two years after the foundation of the city. It is under the management of the Black Nuns. It contains a hospital, a convent, and a church. Eighty of the Sisters are cloistered, and do not go outside of the building and grounds.

In the Notre Dame Hospital the management is decidedly Roman Catholic, but it is open for the relief of the sick and suffering of all creeds; and the patients have the privilege of sending for a clergyman of the denomination they belong to.

The Sisters of the order of Asile de la Providence have eight institutions under their charge at Montreal. They have also charge of the Insane Asylum at Longue Pointe.

EDUCATIONAL INSTITUTIONS.

The school laws in Montreal are, in some respects, peculiar. An assessment of one-fifth of one percent is levied annually upon all the real estate in the city, collected by the City Treasurer with the other taxes, and handed over to the two city boards of Protestant and Catholic School Commissioners. The tax on the property of Protestants goes to the Protestant Board, and that on the property of Catholics to the Catholic Board. One-third of the tax on companies, etc., goes to the Protestant Schools, and two-thirds to the Catholic Schools.

McGILL UNIVERSITY.

The Honorable James McGill was born in Glasgow, October 6, 1744, and died at Montreal, December 19, 1183. By his last will and testament, dated January 8, 1811, he devised that tract and parcel of land commonly called Burnside, situated "near the City of Montreal," and containing about forty-seven acres of land, with the Manor House and other buildings thereon erected, and also bequeathed " the sum of ten thousand pounds current money of the Province of Lower Canada," to the " Royal Institution for the Advancement of Learning," to erect and establish a university or college " for the purposes of education, and the advancement of learning in the Province, with a competent number of professors and teachers to render the establishment effectual and beneficial for the purposes intended ; upon condition also, that one of the Colleges to be comprised in the said University shall be named and perpetually be known and distinguished by the appellation of McGill College."

At the date of the bequest the value of the above-mentioned was estimated at $120,000. Though the charter of McGill University dates from the year 1821, so that it is nominally over eighty years old, its actual history as a teaching institution began somewhat later. Owing to protracted litigation, the property bequeathed did not come into the possession of the Board of Governors until 1829. On the 29th of June in that year, the University was formally opened in

Burnside House, the old residence of the founder.   The Montreal
Medical Institute, which had been in existence for some years, was
incorporated with it as the Faculty of Medicine, and shortly afterwards the Faculty of Arts was established with a Principal and
three Professors.   The infant institution met with several checks to
its growth, and it was not until its charter was amended in 1852,
that it began a career of rapid progress.   Happily for the University, Sir James William Dawson, a distinguished geologist and
naturalist, (born at Pictou, Nova Scotia, in October, 1820) became
its Principal in 1855, and to his unwearied efforts in its behalf in
all its different departments it mainly owes its remarkable success.
Within the last few years its revenues have increased wonderfully—
its staff of teachers is very efficient—and the number of students
prove the value of the varied instruction imparted.   To the faculties of Arts and Medicine those of Law and Applied Science have
been added, and all these are in a most thriving condition.   The
Donalda special course in Arts provides for the education of women
with studies, exemptions, and honors similar to those for men.

The Governors, Principal and Fellows of McGill College consti-
tute the Corporation of the University, and have the power of grant-
ing degrees in all the Arts and Faculties in McGill College, and the
affiliated Colleges of Morrin. Quebec, St. Francis, Richmond, and
Stanstead, P.Q. There are four affiliated Theological Colleges, viz.,
the Congregational, the Presbyterian, the Diocesan, and the Wesleyan, all in Montreal.   The McGill Normal School provides the training requisite for teachers of elementary and model schools and
academies.   The affiliated schools in addition are the Boys'
High School, and the Girls' High School, Montreal, Trafalgar Institute, for the education of women, etc., etc.

Of the numerous noble endowments and benefactions contributed
to the University by the millionaires and other rich men of the city,
it would occupy many pages to give even a brief account.   We need
only mention the William Molson Hall, the Peter Redpath Museum,
the William C. McDonald Physics Building, the Thomas Workman
Department of Mechanical Engineering, the William C. McDonald
Engineering Building, the Library, etc., to show how generously
large sums of money have been presented for University buildings;
and we find that the same liberality has been displayed, especially
of late years, in the endowment of Chairs, Exhibitions and Scholar-

ships, medals and prizes, as also in subscriptions to the general
endowment, subscriptions for current expenses, for the Library,
Museum, and apparatus, and, in fact, for almost everything needed
from time to time in all the faculties.   Ladies and gentlemen vie
with one another in assisting the University with money for any
and every purpose that may be suggested by the universally respect-
ed Principal.   No man in the world has ever labored more
constantly and disinterestedly than he for the permanent benefit of
an educational institution.   He has sacrificed not only income, but
what is more important to him, much time in the drudgery of the
mere routine business of the College.   As he has himself said: "My
connection with this University for the past thirty-eight years has
been fraught with that happiness which results from the conscious-
ness of effort in a worthy cause, and from association with such
noble and self-sacrificing men as have built up McGill College.   But
it has been filled with anxieties and cares, and with continuous and
almost unremitting labor.   I have been obliged to leave undone, or
imperfectly accomplished, many cherished schemes by which I
hoped to benefit humanity, and leave footprints for good on the
sands of time."   These pathetic words must conclude our imperfect
sketch of McGill University and its benefactors.   Principal Peter-
son succeeded Sir Wm. Dawson in 1896.   He has filled the office with
credit to himself and his native country.

The Presbyterian College of Montreal is entirely devoted to the
training of Missionaries and ministers speaking English, French
and Gaelic, in connection with the Presbyterian Church in Canada.

Montreal Wesleyan Theological College was founded in 1872, and
is affiliated to McGill University.   In 1887 it was granted a charter
to confer degrees in Divinity.   The first Principal was the Rev. Geo.
Douglas, LL.D. (1873-1894) who was succeeded by the Rev. W. I.
Shaw, D.D., LL.D. (1895-1900).   The present Principal is the Rev.
J. T. L. Maggs, B.A., D.D., Professor of O. T. Lit.   The other resident
professors are: The Rev. W. I. Shaw, D.D., Prof. of N. T. Lit.; the
Rev. W. Harris, M.A., B.D., Prof. of Church Hist.; the Rev. W. Jack-
son, D.D., Prof. of Syst. Theo., Apologetics, etc.   There are also
instructors in French, Elocution, etc.   The number of registered
students for 1900-1901, resident and non-resident, was thirty-nine.

THE CONGREGATIONAL COLLEGE of Canada was founded in 1839.
In 1864 it became affiliated with McGill University, being the first of

the group of Theological Colleges enjoying this privilege. The officers of instruction are as follows: Rev. J. Henry George, D.D., Ph.D., Principal and Professor of Systematic Theology, Apologetics and Practical Theology. Rev. W. Henry Warriner, M.A. D.D., Registrar and Professor of New Testament Literature, Exegesis and Ecclesiastical Theology. Rev. Harlan Creelman, B.D., Ph.D., Professor of Hebrew, Cognate Languages and Biblical Literature (Miner Foundation.) Lecturers:—Rev. Douglas Mackenzie, D.D., of Chicago Theo. Sem., Philosophy of Religion (McKechnie Lectureship). Rev. Graham Taylor, D.D., of Chicago Theo. Sem., Christian Sociology. Honorable R. S. Weir, D.C.L., Recorder of Montreal, Liturgics and Church Law. Rev. E. M. Hill, M.A., D.D., Pastoral Theology. Mr. John P. Stephen, Instructor in Elocution. Number of Students in Theology, 14; in Preparatory School, 7.

THE SEMINARY OF ST. SULPICE.

On Sherbrooke Street West, commonly called the Montreal College, consists of three departments, the classical, the scientific and the theological. They are commonly designated respectively the Montreal College, Seminary of Philosophy and the Grand Seminary. The Seminary of Philosophy is a magnificent new structure, overlooking Sherbrooke Street, and having its entrance from Cote des Neiges road. In these three courses there are over six hundred and fifty students from all parts of North America, and the Grand Seminary supplies annually more than fifty missionaries for the whole continent. In front of the Grand Seminary are two old towers, or bastions, being all that remains of the ancient "Fort de la Montagne." This mountain fort was in reality a fortified Indian Mission, built in 1694, for the protection of the neophytes against the incursions of their barbarous enemies. The towers, which may be seen from Sherbrooke Street, are thus more than two centuries in existence. They formed the angular bastions of the fort built for the Missionaries, which was a distinct construction from that occupied by the Indians. In one of these towers the Sisters of the Congregation dwelt, and they kept their Indian school in the other.

Laval University.—What the McGill University is to the English and Protestants of the Province, the University of Laval is to the French Catholics. The chief seat of this institution is at Quebec.

The establishment of Laval University at Montreal profoundly agitated the French community, and the matter does not seem to have been finally settled as yet.

St. Mary's College, otherwise called the Jesuits' College, on Bleury Street, is under the management of the Jesuit Fathers.

Ville Marie Convent is the mother house of the order of Sisters of the Congregation. It has accommodation for 1,000 nuns. The nuns of this order make an annual retreat here from all parts of the country. The building is better known to some under the name of Monklands. It was at one time the residence of the Governor-General of Canada. A fine view of the building is got sailing down the river on a clear day. The building was partially destroyed by fire in 1893.

The Sisters of this order at present number about 800 professed Sisters, 90 novices, 50 postulants, and about 20,000 pupils.

The nuns of the order of the Sacred Heart have three establishments in Montreal. The home of the order is at Amiens, France.

The Hochelaga Convent is the mother house of the Sisters of the order of the Holy Names of Jesus and Mary.

The Veterinary College.—Montreal possesses a very important School of Veterinary Science, under the care of Principal McEachran. Students from a great distance come to attend this college. It has six professors besides the principal.

Board of Art Schools.—These are free evening classes for drawing. The Montreal School has 300 pupils.

SCIENCE, LITERATURE AND ARTS.

Libraries.—The principal libraries in Montreal are : the McGill College Library of 25,000 volumes. The Advocates' Library in the Court House, 15,000 vols. Presbyterian College Library, 10,000 vols.

The Mechanics' Institute has a very large library. There is a free public library in the Fraser Institute, Dorchester Street. The Y.M.C.A. has a very good library, and a well supplied free reading room.

The library of the Seminary of St. Sulpice is very large, containing over 30,000 volumes.

THE FINE ARTS.

Music.—There are several musical societies in the city, but only two, the Mendelssohn Choir and Philharmonic Society, are regularly organized.

The Art Association.—This institution owes its existence to the late Bishop Fulford and the late Benaiah Gibb. There is a permanent collection, which is gradually being added to and improved. All art exhibitions of any importance in Montreal take place here. The galleries are open from nine to dusk, and are situated at the corner of St. Catherine Street and Phillips Square. Saturday, except when special exhibitions are in progress, is free.

The Natural History Society.—The Museum of this Society is on University Street, near the English Cathedral. It is well worth a visit. Among the interesting articles to be seen there is the first breech-loading gun ever invented. It was sent to this country by the French Government. It was used by the French in one of their expeditions against the Indians of Lake Oka. The Indians attacked the canoe in which the cannon was placed and upset it. The cannon lay for a while in the bottom of the lake and one part of it was lost there and never found. The finest specimens of mummies to be seen in any museum may be seen there, some of them 3,500 years old, without a hair of the head removed. It contains several valuable relics relating to Canadian history, and several articles of general interest too numerous to be mentioned, such as the scarf of Mary Queen of Scots ; Egyptian sun-dried brick, manufactured, it is supposed, at the time the children of Israel were in bondage there. The best collection extant of Canadian birds is to be seen there.

THE CHATEAU DE RAMEZAY.

This, one of the oldest and most historic buildings in Montreal, is a one-story building, built after the manner of the old Canadian manor houses of unhewn stone and boulders, with pitched roof and vaulted basement.

It is now occupied by the Numismatic and Antiquarian Society as an antiquarian Museum and National portrait gallery.

Claude de Ramezay, who was appointed governor of Montreal in 1703, finding no suitable residence in the then town of fifteen hundred inhabitants, had to build a chateau for himself, and for nearly twenty years occupied this chateau, which took the name of de Ramezay after its owner, as his official residence as commandant of the troops. Here, in the Council Chamber, he made plans for the defense of the Colony from the raids of the Indians from the West and the " Bostonnais" to the south.

In 1745 the property passed into the hands of " La Compagnie des Indes." (The India Company), and under its ownership was for twenty-five years the chief lieu of the Canadian fur trade. From this occupation it was long known as the " India House."

As the Conquest had dissolved the company as far as Canadian business was concerned, the building was sold in 1764 to William Grant, who leased it in 1774 to the Government, to be again the official residence of the Governor of Montreal. So, in 1775, when the Continental army captured Montreal, they took up their head-quarters here and Generals Montgomery, Wooster and Benedict Arnold, successively held councils in the old Council Chamber, and in the same chamber the Commissioners, Franklin, Chase and Carrollton, appointed by Congress, held council as to the best means of gaining possession of Canada.

When the Government purchased the house in 1778, its designation was changed to " The Government House," which title it bore as long as it was the residence of the governors. The Special Council appointed in 1838 to legislate for the Province of Lower Canada, sat here, until superseded by the Parliament of the Dominion of Canada, elected in 1840. In 1845, when the seat of government was removed to Montreal, it became the departmental office, and it was here, in 1849, that Lord Elgin was mobbed after having given assent to the Rebellion Loss Bill.

After the removal of the seat of government from Montreal in 1850, it was successively occupied as a court house, a normal school, a college and again as a court house.

SPORTS.

In Canada fondness for outdoor sports has been a characteristic of the people, and in no town or city has it shown more vitality than in the City of the " Royal Mount," the commercial metropolis of the Dominion. Canadians have inherited the three fascinating out-door pastimes of Lacrosse, Snowshoeing, and Tobogganing from the Indians.

The M.A.A.A. (Montreal Amateur Athletic Association) is the centre of all sorts of sport in Montreal. Their building and gymnasium is at 149-153 Mansfield Street, and grounds at Westmount.

CURLING.

The Montreal Curling Club, founded in 1807, is the oldest club of organized out-door sport on the continent.

The other clubs are the "Thistle," organized in 1843, the Caledonia, organized in 1850, the Heather, organized in 1887, and the St. Lawrence, organized in 1891.

CRICKET.

The early records of cricket in Montreal have yet to be traced. The first international match with the United States was played in Montreal in 1845.

Toronto Cricket Clubs in 1846 and 1849.

SNOWSHOEING.

The Montreal Snowshoe Club, or the "Old Tuque Bleu" dates back to 1840. In 1862 the members assisted to form the Victoria Rifles. In 1869 H. R. H. Prince Arthur, now Duke of Connaught, then serving as a lieutenant in the Prince Consort Rifle Brigade, attended the club race meeting and honored the club by allowing his name to be placed upon the roll as an Honorary Life Member.

In 1874 the "Emerald," and shortly afterwards the "St. George" Snowshoe Clubs were formed, and the "Le Canadien," in 1878, and the "Argyle,' in 1880.

To the "Old Tuque Bleu" belongs the lion's share of the organization and success of each successive winter carnival.

LACROSSE.

The early records of the "National Game" in Montreal are somewhat obscure. As far as can be ascertained at present, the first recorded match was played between teams of Iroquois and Algonquin Indians in September, 1834, at the St. Pierre Race Course.

The first annual meeting of the pioneer club of lacrosse, and the "Alma Mater" of the National Game, was held in September, 1857, and the next club of white players to organize was the "Hochelaga," in 1858, which eventually amalgamated with the Montreal, in March, 1860, under the name of "The Lacrosse Club of Montreal," which was changed to the "Montreal Lacrosse Club," in March, 1861. The first rules and laws of the game were compiled and published by Dr. Geo. W. Beers, (the now Hon. President of the Montreal Club) in 1860. The Shamrock Lacrosse Club was formed in 1867.

SKATING.

The "Montreal Skating Club" was formed in 1859, and erected a skating rink on St. Urbain Street. The club has now a large skating rink on Drummond Street.

FOOTBALL.

The "Montreal Football Club," which has the honor of being the pioneer club of Canada, was founded in 1868. It is affiliated with the M.A.A.A. since 1885.

TOBOGGANING.

As an organized sport Tobogganing is one of recent date and is already fast on the incline and decline. The first Montreal club was established in 1881. During the Winter Carnivals of 1883, '84 and '85 this sport was very popular, and a number of artificial slides were erected in different parts of the city. The only slide now standing is that on the Mountain Park. This ridiculous and dangerous amusement is now chiefly practiced by the small children, who take possession without permission of most of the streets suitable to their amusement, much to the annoyance and danger of the pedestrians.

Hockey on ice is a game which the youth of Canada has developed for himself. In Scotland or Ireland "hockey" or "shinty," is a field game, but in Canada it has developed into one of the most fascinating of winter sports, rivalling lacrosse in the intensity of interest. The first recorded match was played in the Victoria Rink on March 3rd, 1875. In 1877 appears the first mention of rules of the game.

BICYCLING.

Bicycling may be said to date its birth from 1865, when Pierre Lallement, a French mechanic, invented a two-wheel cycle with a foot crank, at Ansonia, Connecticut, and rode from that town to New Haven. The first complete bicycle introduced on this continent was brought across the Atlantic in June, 1874, by Mr. A. T. Lane, ex-president of the Canadian Wheelman's Association, and on Dominion Day of the same year Mr. Lane rode through the streets of Montreal, the first bicycle seen running on the streets on this continent. Bicycling is now such that many sincerely wish that as an amusement it may be as short lived as tobogganing, or that its devotees may take the notion to exchange the crowded streets and squares of the city for the long country roads.

Theatres.—The Academy, on Victoria Street. The Queen's, corner of Victoria and St. Catherine Streets. The Royal, on Coté Street.

Hunting.—Montreal can boast of the best conducted hunting establishment on this continent; Kennels, on Papineau Road.

Gymnasium.—The Gymnasium of the Montreal Amateur Athletic Association (M.A.A.), 114 Mansfield Street, is a very good and useful institution.

The following kinds of amusements are also well represented at Montreal:—Baseball, Chess, Boating, Golf, Racket, Lawn Tennis. (Racing—Blue Bonnets, about five miles west of Montreal, and Lepine Park, about 3 miles east of Montreal, are the principal places for this amusement, where vast crowds of people gather on a racing day.)

Militia.—Volunteering is a favorite occupation of the young men of the city. There are six regiments of infantry, one troop of Cavalry, one company of Engineers, one battery of Horse Artillery, and six batteries of Garrison Artillery.

MONTREAL AMATEUR ATHLETIC ASSOCIATION.

INCORPORATED 1881.

Past Presidents:—A.W. Stevenson, Wm. L. Maltby, Angus Grant, F. C. A. McIndoe, Jas. A. Taylor, Thos. L. Paton, Major Freeman.

The Association is composed of the following Clubs :—

Montreal Lacrosse Club, organized 1856.

Montreal Snowshoe Club, organized 1840.

Montreal Bicycle Club, organized 1878.

Montreal Toboggan Club, organized 1883.

Montreal Football Club, organized 1868.

The Gymnasium, Club Rooms and office are owned by the Association, and are situated at 149 Mansfield Street, central to both the business and residential portions of the city. The Association also is in possession of one of the finest athletic grounds on the continent, containing over ten acres of ground, and beautifully situated on St. Catherine Street West, in the wealthy residential suburb of Westmount.

NEWSPAPERS AND PERIODICALS.

The first newspaper published in Canada was the Halifax *Gazette*, published by John Bushnell, 23rd March, 1752. There are now about fifty newspapers and periodicals in English and French. There are three French and four English daily newspapers and ten French and eight English weekly newspapers, eight French and eleven English monthlies and two English quarterlies.

The *Gazette* (Conservative) is the only English morning paper in Montreal, and claims unbroken connection with the first newspaper published in the old Chateau de Ramesay under the direction of the famous Benjamin Franklin, in 1778. It was originally written in French, with the object of persuading the French-Canadians to form Lower Canada into a State of the Union. It was next written half in French and half in English, but, after a short experiment, it was finally printed all in English. From a layman's point of view the *Gazette* is the best all-round paper in Montreal.

The *Star* is first and foremost a newspaper. It is safe to say that no other newspaper in Canada can compete with it in the matter of getting most news in least time. It has the largest circulation of any English newspaper in Canada. It was established in 1869. Its weekly edition has a circulation of nearly a quarter of a million.

The *Herald* is the local English Liberal organ. It had the misfortune to be three times burned out. It is now very ably managed, and is holding its own end up well. It is a lively, interesting newspaper, very suitable for the seaside.

The Montreal *Witness* was founded in 1845. It has grown from a very small weekly to a great modern daily, and that without sacrificing any of the principles of Christian righteousness with which it was started by the late Mr. John Dougall. The *Witness* aims to print all the news that is fit to print, and comments on the same in honest, intelligent and vigorous editorials. It is entirely free from partisan and financial influence, and perhaps no other publication holds so high a place in the esteem and regard of the Canadian people. It guards its advertising columns with the same zealous care as its news ; and advertisements of a doubtful or hurtful nature are strictly excluded. The position occupied by the 'Witness' in Canadian journalism for the past half century has indeed been an honored one, and it is little wonder then that it has so many warm friends. The paper is now conducted by Mr. John Redpath Dougall, a son of the founder, and by Mr. Frederick E. Dougall, a grandson of the founder.

La Presse, founded in 1884, is a very substantial monument of the literary and business ability of French Canadian citizens. Not only has it left behind all other French newspapers, but it claims the largest circulation in Canada in any language. Like the *Star* it is first and foremost simply a newspaper.

La Patrie (French) was originally established as a Liberal and Republican advocate by Ex-Mayor Beaugrand. Since the advent of the Laurier Government into power this paper has become the property of the Tarte family, with possibly some English-speaking shareholders. It is first and foremost the personal organ of Mr. Tarte, the Minister of Public Works in the Dominion Government. I have supported the Laurier Government at the last two elections. In common with many others of both political parties, I have strong objections to the Minister of Public Works and his organ. I object to the compulsory eviction of any people from the land, whether they are Irish tenants, Scotch crofters, French Acadians or Anticosti settlers. Mr. Tarte and his personal organ *La Patrie*, advocated the forcible eviction of the Anticosti settlers, therefore I object to Mr. Tarte and his organ, and will continue to do so. I may say here that I deny the right of any hereditary aristocracy to levy rent from land they have never cultivated. I therefore deny the right of Mr. Menier to the Island of Anticosti, or the right of any one to sell it to him. In fact, I deny the right of any man anywhere to the sole ownership of such an extensive tract of land. Upholding such views, I cannot be expected to be very friendly to any minister of any Crown upholding Mr. Menier's preposterous pretensions in the matter of Anticosti. In future, I will, therefore, oppose not only Mr. Tarte, but any government that proposes to give him a portfolio. For next election, therefore, the question will be, " Will Tarte go or will the whole Laurier Government go?" Many like myself supported the Laurier government at the last election chiefly on account of their antagonism to the ex-leader (Tupper) and the foolish methods of the chief Conservative agitators. This is not a question of French and English as some foolishly and wickedly have made politics in Canada. Many men of French origin, both

in Canada and old France, have been some of the ablest and best
men that the sun ever shone on.   It is not a question of loyalty to
Britain and British institutions, for some British institutions, such
as landlordism and hereditary aristocra:y and church establishments
in England, Scotland and Wales need abolition altogether to reform
them.   The want of a leader in Great Britain to take up these two
great questions is the cause of the weakness of the present Liberal
party in Great Britain.   It is not a question between Republicanism
and Monarchy, for our present King, with all his experience, wide
family connections, and good common sense, is of far more use to
us as an Empire than any other man raised from the ranks would
be, under the present circumstances.   But we ought to give the
farmers in England, Ireland, Scotland and Wales, freehold of their
lands, and abolish dual ownership, and nationalize the railways,
coal, gold, silver and iron mines, as well as the post-office.

Le Journal (French), a new Conservative organ, started in 1899.
It is a morning daily.

World Wide, a weekly budget of literary selections.

The True Witness is the Irish Catholic National and Home Rule
organ.

The Shareholder, published in Montreal, is a very valuable paper
to business men.

L'Aurore (French Protestant organ).

Canadian Antiquarian and Numismatic Journal, published quarterly.

Canadian Journal of Commerce.

Canadian Journal of Fabrics, published monthly, and the *Canadian
Textile Directory*, published by Mr. R. B. Biggar, Fraser Building, St.
Sacrament Street.

Canadian Record of Science, quarterly.

Church Guardian, published weekly in the interests of the Church
of England, by Mr. L. H. Davidson, 190 St. James Street.

Canadian Medical Record, monthly.

Educational Record, monthly.

Insurance and Finance Chronicle, published monthly by R. W.
Smith, 1724 Notre Dame Street.

Legal News, published weekly at the *Gazette* office.

Lovell's Montreal Directory, published every year, price, $5.00.

Lovell's Montreal Business Directory, $1.50.

Lower Canada Jurist, monthly.

Montreal Law Reports, monthly.

Montreal Produce Bulletin, weekly.

Northern Messenger, weekly.

Presbyterian Record, monthly.

The Real Estate Record, monthly, indispensable to every one interested in real estate in Montreal. J. C. Simpson & Co., 181 St. James Street.

Trade Bulletin.

Montreal Medical Journal, monthly.

The Trade Review, weekly.

Presbyterian College Journal, published monthly during each session, is considered the leading journal of the kind in Canada.

University Gazette, published weekly during the session by the students of McGill College.

HISTORICAL TABLETS.

No. 1.—Metcalfe, near Sherbrooke, site of a large Indian village, claimed to be the town of Hochelaga visited by Jacques Cartier in 1535.

No. 2.—(Not located.) To the Hon. John Molson, the father of steam navigation on the St. Lawrence. He launched the steamer "Accommodation" for Montreal and Quebec service.

No. 3.—On Custom House Square. "The first Public Square of Montreal, 1657—La place du marché—granted by the Seigneurs 1676."

Nos. 4 and 5.—Front of Custom House. This site was selected and named in 1611 "La Place Royale," by Samuel de Champlain, the founder of Canada. Near this spot on the 18th day of May, 1642, landed the founders of Montreal, commanded by Paul de Chomedy, "Sieur de Maisonneuve." The first proceeding was a (mass) religious service.

No. 6.—On Port Sreet. Here was the Fort of Ville Marie, built 1643, demolished 1648, and replaced by the House of Monsieur de Callières, 1686.

No. 7.—On Foundling Street. Site of the Chateau of Louis Hector de Calliers, Governor of Montreal, 1684; of New France 1698-1703. He terminated the fourteen years' war with the Iroquois by treaty at Montreal, 1701.

No. 8.—Corner of St. Paul and St. Sulpice. Here was the first parish Church of Ville Marie, erected in 1656.

No. 9.—On Seminary wall, Notre Dame Street.   The second parish Church of Ville Marie, built in 1672, dedicated 1678, and demolished in 1829, occupied the middle of Notre Dame Street.

Nos. 10 and 11.—On the Seminary Building.   " The Seminary of St. Sulpice, founded at Paris by M. Jean Jacques Olier, 1641, established at Ville Marie, 1657 ; M. Gabriel de Queylus, superior, Seigneurs of the Island of Montreal, 1663."

" François Dollier de Casson, first historian of Montreal, Captain under Marshal de Fournier, then priest of St. Sulpice during 35 years.   He died in 1701, curé of the Parish.

No. 12.—St. Helen near Notre Dame.   Here stood until 1866 the Church and Monastery of the Recollet Fathers, 1692, in which the Anglicans from 1764 to 1789, and the Presbyterians from 1791 to 1792 worshipped.

No. 13.—On the Imperial Building (107 St. James Street).   Near this square, afterwards named La Place d'Armes, the founders of Ville Marie first encountered the Iroquois, whom they defeated, Chomedy de Maisonneuve killing the Indian Chief with his own hands, 3rd March, 1644.

No. 14.—Corner Notre Dame and McGill.   " Recollet Gate":   By this gate Amherst took possession 8th September, 1760.   General Hull, U.S.; 25 officers and 300 men entered as prisoners of war, 20th September, 1812.

No. 15.—Corner Notre Dame and Jacques Cartier Square.   The residence of the Hon. James McGill, founder of McGill University, 1744-1873.

Nos. 16 and 17.—On Chateau de Ramezay, opposite City Hall. Chateau de Ramezay, built about 1705, by Claude de Ramezay, Governor of Montreal, 1703.   Headquarters of La Compagnie des Indes, 1745.   Official residence of the British Governors after the conquest. Headquarters of the American Army, 1775, and of Special Council, 1837.

In 1775 this Chateau was the headquarters of the American General Wooster, and here in 1776, under General Benedict Arnold, the Commissioners of Congress, Benjamin Franklin, Samuel Chase and Charles Carroll, of Carrolton, held council.

No. 18. — Notre Dame near St. Lambert Hill.   Site of Christ Church Cathedral, the first Anglican Church, 1814, burnt 1856.

No. 19.—On Hotel Dieu Building. Hotel Dieu de Ville Marie, founded in 1644 by Jeanne Mance. Transferred 1861 to this land given by Gabriel and Benoît Bassett. Removal of remains of Jeanne Mance and 168 nuns in 1861.

No. 20.—Sherbrooke Street, near Montreal College, marking the headquarters of General Amherst at the time of the surrender of Montreal to the British power.

No. 21.—Notre Dame Street, east of St. Lambert Hill. In 1694 here stood the house of La Mothe Cadillac, the founder of Detroit.

No. 22.—Corner of Sherbrooke and Park Ave, Major-General, James Murray, Brigade Commander under Wolfe at Quebec, 1759, and afterwards first British Governor of Canada, encamped on this plateau with the second division of Amherst's army upon the surrender of Montreal and all Canada, 8th September, 1760.

No. 23.—Dollard Lane (at 226 St. James). To Adam Dollard des Ormeau, who with 16 colonists, 4 Algonquins, and 1 Huron, sacrificed their lives at the Long Sault of the Ottawa, and saved the Colony.

No. 24.—On the Bonsecours Market. Sir William Johnson, of Johnson Hall, on the Mohawk River, the celebrated superintendent of Indian affairs, the first American Baronet, commanded the Indian allies with Amherst's army in 1660. To them was issued in commemoration the first British Montreal medals. Here stood the house of his son, Sir John Johnson, Indian Commissioner.

No. 25.—On St. Paul Street, opposite Bonsecours Market. Site of the house of General Ralph Burton, second Governor of Montreal 1763. He executed on the Plains of Abraham at Wolfe's dying command the military operation which finally decided the day.

No. 26.—On Dalhousie Square Fire Station. To Brigadier-General Thomas Gage, second in command under Amherst, first British Governor of Montreal, 1760. Afterwards last British governor of Massachusetts, 1775.

No. 27.—Near head of Simpson Street. Site of the residence of Sir Alexander Mackenzie, discoverer of Mackenzie River, 1793, the first European to cross the Rocky Mountains.

No. 28.—Corner Notre Dame and St. Peter Streets. Forrestier House; here General Montgomery resided during the winter of 1775-76.

No. 29.—Corner of Dorchester and Bleury. This street was

named in honor of Sir Guy Carleton, Lord Dorchester, commander
of the British forces and preserver of the colony during the American invasion 1775-76 ; twice Governor of Canada, by whom the
Quebec Act, 1774, was obtained.

No. 30.—On St. Paul Street, near Bonsecours Market.   The
Papineau House ; six of their generations have dwelt here.

No. 31.—On Gault Bro.'s Warehouse (site of the old First Baptist
Chapel), St. Helen Street.   "This tablet commemorates the organization on this site of the first Young Men's Christian Association
on the American continent, November 25, 1851.   Erected on the
occasion of the Jubilee celebration, June 8th, 1901."

AUTHORITIES CONSULTED.

The following authorities were consulted in compiling this book:
Handbook of the Dominion (Dawson's), Montreal Past and Present
(George Bishop & Co.), All Round Route (Canada News Co.), A B C
Railway Guide and Starke's Almanac (Theo. Robinson), " Reminis-
cences of my Visit to the Grey Nunnery," (for sale there), History
of Notre Dame de Lourdes (for sale by the Sisters of Notre Dame
de Lourdes), Historical Sketches of Notre Dame of Montreal (for
sale at the church). Our Caughnawagas in Egypt (W. Drysdale &
Co.), History of the Montreal Prison (J. D. Borthwick), The
Montreal Herald, McNally's Pocket Cyclopaedia, Hayden's Dictionary
of Dates, Montreal Directory, 1890-91, C.P.R. Timetable, with notes;
Appleton's Canadian Guide Book, George Murray, Sights and
Shrines of Montreal, by G. W. Lighthall ; Our City and Our Sports.
Montreal Directory, 1819.

For the historical account of the origin of the names of the
streets I am indebted to a paper contributed by Mr. Woodly, of Cote
St. Antoine (a boy 13 years old), to the *Witness*, and also for information gathered from the Rev. Mr. Borthwick's contribution to the
Star on the same subject.

For the benefit of readers of this book, who may wish to get
some information about other places outside of Montreal, I may
state that after perusing all the publications I could get my hand
on in this line, I know of no more useful book than Appleton's
Canadian Guide Book.   The Appletons were fortunate in securing
the services of Prof. Roberts, of King's College, Nova Scotia. who
is recognized, on all hands, as the best versed in Canadian literature
of our living authors.

SUBURBS AND NEIGHBORING TOWNS AND VILLAGES.

[N.B.—The distance is calculated from the Post-Office.]

CAUGHNAWAGA, an Indian village opposite Lachine.

COTEAU ST. LOUIS.—Two miles from Montreal, east of Mount Royal, has large stone quarries. Population about 3,500.

COTEAU ST. PIERRE.—On the upper Lachine Road, three miles from Montreal; has large brick works. Population about 300.

COTE ST. LUC.—Three miles from Montreal, on the Lachine Road. Population, 250.

COTE ST. PAUL.—Three miles from Montreal, on the Lower Lachine Road. Population about 2,000.

COTE VISITATION.—On Papineau Road, two miles east of Montreal. Population about 600.

HUNTINGDON.—Huntingdon stands in more close relation to Montreal than any other outside town in the Dominion. Montreal is particularly interested in the welfare of Huntingdon, and Huntingdon is particularly interested in the welfare of Montreal. When the Huntingdon people want anything that they have not got themselves, they don't go to Ottawa or Toronto (as others that might be mentioned), they come to Montreal. Huntingdon is a thriving little town, surrounded by a fine farming country, and the centre of the chief settlement of the English-speaking people in south-western Quebec. The Huntingdon district (as it is commonly called) is renowned for its cheese and Clydesdale horses. Its thrifty farmers are always the best customers of city merchants. Huntingdon village has two industries that do it credit. First, the well-known establishment of Daniel Boyd & Co., where all kinds of agricultural implements are manufactured, such as ploughs, harrows, reapers, and mowing machines, hay-presses and other articles too numerous to mention in a short notice of this kind. Boyd & Co. are also agents for the famous Waterous Engine Works, Brantford, Ontario. Boyd & Co. are the only manufacturers of the Dederick Hay Presses in this section, and do a large trade in them. Huntingdon has two railways, the Grand Trunk and the St. Lawrence & Adirondack, with 14 trains daily. Its excellent facilities of communication have increased the attendance at its celebrated academy, which at the last A.A. examination obtained first place both for competitors over and under 18 years of age. The local newspaper is the well-known

Gleaner, whose editor, Mr. Sellar, is recognized as one of the best authorities in Canada on anything relating to Canadian history. The Huntingdon annual exhibition is always a success.

LACHINE.—Nine miles from Montreal, is one of the favorite summer resorts in the neighborhood of Montreal. It is the principal boating place in the vicinity of Montreal. There are regattas on the lake opposite the town annually. At Lachine the boats shooting the rapids always connect with the Montreal trains, morning and evening, during summer, for the excursionists who come to shoot the rapids, many of whom come a long distance on purpose. Shooting the Lachine Rapids of late years is something like going to see Niagara Falls. The population is about 5,000.

LAPRAIRIE.—A village on the South side of the River St. Lawrence, nine miles south-west of Montreal. Population about 2,000. During the summer season the ferry boat makes three trips a day to Montreal and back. The first railway in British North America was constructed from here to St. John, in 1836. It was discontinued and the rails taken up a few years after. The best hotel is the Montreal House.

LONGUEUIL.—On the south side of the St. Lawrence, opposite Hochelaga. Some years ago a railway was run on the ice across the river from Montreal to Longueuil. Population, 3,500.

LONGUE POINTE.—Six miles east of Montreal, known now throughout the world as the site of the lunatic asylum, which was burned, in which many human beings were burned to cinders. The exact number is not known. Population, about 800.

MAISONNEUVE.—East of Hochelaga, about four miles from Montreal. Population, about 1,350.

MONTREAL JUNCTION.—A new village on the C. P. R. Montreal and Toronto line, five miles from Montreal. Population, about 200.

MOUNT ROYAL AVENUE lies east of Mount Royal, at the terminus of the street railway. Population, about 400.

MOUNT ROYAL VALE, off Cote St. Luc Road. Population, about 150.

NOTRE DAME DE GRACE.—A small village at the back of the Mountain. Population, about 400.

NOTRE DAME DES NEIGES lies in rear of Mount Royal. Population about 800.

OUTREMONT lies at the west end of Mount Royal. Population about 1,200.

PETIT VILLAGE TURCOT, near Cote St. Paul. Population, about 200.

SAULT AU RECOLLET is near the east end of the island of Montreal, about seven miles from the city. Population, about 400.

ST. CUNEGONDE.—An old town joined to the west end of Montreal, with a corporation of its own. Population, about 12,000.

ST. LAMBERT.—A town on the south side of the St. Lawrence, opposite Montreal at the end of Victoria Bridge. Population, about 1,500.

ST. LOUIS DU MILE END, formerly part of Cote St. Louis, has a population of about 10,000.

WESTMOUNT is principally inhabited by Montreal business men. It is at the western terminus of the St. Catharine Street line of the street railway. Population, about 9,500.

MONKLANDS, formerly the residence of the Governors of Canada, now occupied by nuns who call it Villa Maria, is located here. The convent was nearly destroyed by fire in 1893. Fortunately there were no lives lost; but the financial loss of the sisters was very heavy and only partially covered by insurance.

ST. HENRY is an incorporated town with a population of about 10,000. It is about three miles west of Montreal.

VERDUN, formerly called Lower Lachine Road, is about five miles west of Montreal, on the banks of the St. Lawrence. The new Protestant Insane Asylum is built here. A ferry crosses from here to La Tortue, a small village on the other side of the river.

HOW TO VISIT THE PRINCIPAL PLACES OF INTEREST IN THE SHORTEST TIME FOR THE LEAST MONEY.

In whatever quarter of the city you are lodging, the first place to visit is Notre Dame Church.

From the Windsor, if you do not wish to hire a cab, you may get an electric car at the door to take you near the Post-Office, and then a few paces from you is Notre Dame Church and several other places of interest. A few blocks east from there is the new City Hall, the Court House, Nelson's Monument, St. Gabriel Street old Presbyterian Church, and not far away is the Bonsecours Market and Bonsecours Church. While there you may visit the Harbor and the new Custom House about half a mile further west. Then walk

up McGill Street, to Victoria Square, from whence you may get the
street cars to take you to the principal places of interest up-town.
First visit the Notre Dame de Lourdes, near the corner of St. Catherine and St. Denis Streets. From thence, retrace your steps
westward till you come to Bleury Street, and there is the old Jesuits
Church and College. Then turn up to St. Catherine Street west,
till you come to the Art Gallery, corner of Phillips Square. Then
visit the English Cathedral and the Museum, of the Natural History
Society. Take the street cars till you come west as far as Guy
Street and visit the Grey Nunnery at noon. After dinner hire a
cab to take you to McGill College (there is a very interesting
museum in connection with the College, which the visitor may enter
on payment of a small entrance fee), and close by are the two city
reservoirs; and if you don't wish to hire a cab to take you to the
top of the mountain, you can go up by the elevator for five cents.
Then, after you have taken a good view of the surrounding country
from the top of the mountain, and visited the two cemeteries, you
can come back to the city by the street cars, and you have a day
well spent, and not over a dollar of necessary expense, besides your
hotel bill.

BANKS.

Bank of Montreal.—See Page 8.

Canadian Bank of Commerce, Canada Life Bldg., cor. St. James
and St. Peter Streets, A. M. Crombie, Local Manager.

Merchants' Bank of Canada, 205 St. James Street. Andrew
Allan, President ; Geo. Hague, General Manager.

Merchants' Bank of Halifax, Notre Dame Street.

Bank of British North America, 140 St. James Street. H. Stike-
man, General Manager.

Quebec Bank, New York Life Building. T. McDougall, Local
Manager.

The Molson Bank, 200 St. James Street.

Bank of Toronto, 168 St. James Street.

Ontario Bank, 8 Place d'Armes. R. N. King, Local Manager.

Union Bank of Canada, 1664 Notre Dame Street. C. H. Balfour,
Local Manager.

Bank of Nova Scotia, 130 St. James Street.

Banque d'Hochelaga, 107 St. James Street.

Banque Nationale, 101 St. James Street.

ORIGIN OF THE NAMES OF SOME OF THE STREETS.

The first names given to the streets of old Montreal were given by Mr. Dollier de Casson, the Superior of the Seminary, the priests of the Seminary being the seigneurs of Montreal.

Amherst Street was named in honor of General Amherst. Some of his exploits were the taking of Louisburg from the French in 1758. He was engaged in the capture of Quebec, and compelled the capitulation of Montreal in 1760.

Aylmer Street was named after Lord Aylmer, who was Governor-General of Canada in 1831.

Champlain Street was named after Samuel de Champlain, the famous explorer. He founded Quebec in 1608. He was the first Governor of Canada in 1633.

Common Street is so called on account of the common pasturage for cattle along the banks of the river in that locality in the olden times.

Craig Street was named after Sir James Craig, who was Governor of Canada from 1807 to 1811. In the olden times a creek ran where Craig street now is. There were several wooden bridges across the creek where the street cars now run.

Dollard Lane was called after Dollard, a French Commander, who made himself famous in the wars between the French and the Indians.

Dorchester Street was called after Sir Guy Carleton, Governor-General of Canada, after the British conquest. He was governor from 1796 to 1797.

Fortification Lane was called after the old fortification wall, the north side of which was built on that site.

Frontenac Street was called in honor of the popular French Governor of Canada of that name. He was governor from 1672 to 1682. He built Fort Frontenac, now called Kingston.

Gosford Street was named after the Earl of Gosford, who was Governor-General in 1835.

McGill Street was called after the Hon. James McGill, the founder of McGill University, and the first English-speaking Mayor of Montreal.

Maisonneuve Street was named after Monsieur de Maisonneuve, the founder of Montreal.

Metcalfe Street was called after Lord Metcalfe, Governor-General in 1842.

Montcalm Street was named after the famous French General Montcalm, who fell on the Plains of Abraham, when Quebec was taken in 1759.

Murray Street, named after General Murray, the first Governor-General of Canada after the Conquest.

Papineau Road was named after the Hon. L. J. Papineau, the leader of the French-Canadian Rebellion in 1837.

Richmond Street was named after the Duke of Richmond, who was Governor in 1818 and 1819. He died on the 29th August, 1819, from the effects of the bite of a pet fox.

Sherbrooke Street was called after Sir John Cope Sherbrooke, who was Governor in 1816 and 1818.

Wolfe Street was named after General Wolfe, the hero of the capture of Quebec in 1759.

GUIDE TO THE PRINCIPAL STREETS.

The numbers on the streets run from east to west, and from the river towards the mountain, or north and south.

The principal Streets of the city, running east and west, are:— Wellington, William, Commissioners, St. Paul, Notre Dame, (about five miles in length from Hochelaga to St. Henry, the east end of which was formerly called St. Mary and the west end St. Joseph Street; these three streets are now under the name of one street). St. James Street; the west end of this street was formerly called St. Bonaventure Street. Osborne is a continuation of Lagauchetiere. Craig and St. Antoine Streets are continuations one of the other. Lagauchetiere, St. Catherine, Dorchester, Mignonne, Ontario and Sherbrooke Streets. A large portion of the dwellings of the upper classes of Montreal are on this last street. Latour, Jurors, and Vitre form one street.

The principal streets running from the river towards the Mountain are St. Denis, St. Lawrence Main. St. Peter, Bleury and Park Avenue are a continuation one of the other. Bonsecours is a continuation of St. Denis Street towards Bonsecours Market. St. Elizabeth Street and Laval Avenue are a continuation one of the other. Cadieux Street is a continuation of St. Constant Street. St. Dominique Street. St. Urbain Street is a continuation of St. Sulpice

Street. Mance Street is a continuation of St. George Street. McGill Street. University Street. Metcalfe Street is a continuation of Cathedral Street. Peel Street is a continuation of Windsor Street. Mountain Street.

The following streets have different names at different parts. The question of having a single name for them has been long under discussion : — Mountain and McCord, Hanover and University; St. Peter, Bleury and Park Avenue; Berthelet, Ontario and Burnside Place ; Champ de Mars and Rousseau ; College and St. Paul ; William and Foundling ; Latour, Jurors and Vitre; St. George and Mance; St. Constant and Cadieux; St. Lambert and St. Lawrence; Bonsecours and St. Denis; Gosford and Sanguinet; Monarque and Papineau Road; Port and St. Nicholas; Callieres and St. Francois Xavier; Windsor and Peel; Cathedral, Metcalfe and McTavish; Brunswick and Union Avenue; St. Elizabeth and Laval Avenue; St. Charles Borrommee, Arcade and Mitchison Avenue; Guy and Cote des Neiges Road; Quiblier and Tupper; Comte and Lincoln Avenue; Longueuil Ferry and St. Suzanne; Pantaleon and German.

SPECIAL NOTICES.

John Lovell & Son have published their thirteenth edition of Lovell's Business Directory, containing an index to streets, tariff of Customs, and names, business and address of every firm or person doing business in Montreal. It is corrected up to July, 1900. A miscellaneous directory has been compiled with great care and adds to the book's worth. A guide to streets will serve as a handy reference. The binding is tasty and reliable. In board, the Directory sells for $1.50—400 pages.

O. L. FULLER, Advertising Agent, Lovell's Montreal Directory. Advertisements prepared and placed in any medium anywhere; 25 years' experience. Office, 112 Selby, Westmount. House same address.

DAVID WATERS, 494 St. James Street. Established 1876. Largest stock in Canada of scarce and standard Canadian and American new and second-hand books, steel engravings, water colors and oil paintings. Highest cash prices paid for clean and complete works, paper cover novels and general literature; also antique mahogany furniture, ancient silverware, brass goods, old pistols, guns, swords and other objects of antiquity.

PETER LYALL & SONS.—The finest built and the most architecturally beautiful city on the continent is Montreal.   The greatest credit is due to the architects and builders of the city; and in the foreground of building contractors stands the celebrated firm of Messrs. Peter Lyall & Sons, whose achievements as builders stand out prominently not only all over the Metropolis, but all over the Dominion.   Mr. Peter Lyall established this business in 1875, after having acquired a wide range of practical experience both in his native country of Scotland and in Canada.   Deeds speak louder than words, and we cannot record the achievements of this celebrated firm in a better way than by mentioning a few of the substantial monuments of their work, such as—The Royal Victoria Hospital, Royal Insurance Building, Macdonald Engineering Building, New York Life Insurance Building, New Star Building, and New Grand Trunk Offices.

WIGHTON, MORRISON & Co.—In the same category as Peter Lyall & Sons, just mentioned, comes another famous firm of building contractors—Wighton, Morrison & Co. — who are also leaving substantial monuments of their skill, as may be seen at a glance at the following out of many other buildings they have put up—Greenshields, on Victoria Square; Mining and Chemistry Building, at McGill ; Bank of Toronto, new Galt Mills, at Valleyfield; Birks' Building, St. Catherine Street; Redpath Library Building, Canada Jute Co. Buildings, and various other buildings too numerous to mention in a short complimentary notice.

INDEX TO STREETS.

Conde, off 479 Wellington.
Congregation, off 384 Wellington.
Contant, off 84 Campeau.
Conway, off 25 St. Etienne.
Costigan Lane, off 363 Richmond.
Cote Ave., off 304 Sanguinet.
Cote des Neiges Road, off 1227 Sherbrooke.
Cote, off 581 Craig.
Coursol, off 158 Canning.
Courville, now a part of Prince Arthur.
Craig, continuation of St. Antoine East.
Crescent, off 952 Dorchester.
Cuvillier, off 178 Notre Dame.
Cypress, off 150 Peel.
Dalhousie, off 128 William.
Dalhousie Square, at 1410 Notre Dame.
D'Argenson, off 590 St. Patrick.
Darling, off 199 Notre Dame.
Davidson, off 191 Notre Dame.
De Bresoles, off 43 St. Sulpice.
Delisle, off 96 Canning.
Delorimier Ave., formerly Colborne Ave., off 893 Notre Dame.
Demontigny, formerly Mignonne, off 227 St. Urbain.
Desalaberry, off 1119 Notre Dame.
Desery, off 257 Notre Dame.
Desrivieres, off 46 St. Antoine.
Desrivieres Ave., off 0 Desrivieres.
Devienne, off 227 St. George.
Dollard, off 224 St. James.
Dominion, off 2077 Notre Dame.
Dominion Ave., off 84 Dominion.
Dominion Square, on Windsor, Peel and Metcalfe.
Donegana, off 26 Windsor.
Dorchester, a leading street, east to west, below St. Catherine.
Dowd, formerly St. Germain, off 90 Bleury.
Drolet, off 13 St. Louis Square.
Drummond, off 2450 St. Catherine.
Dubord, off 37 Sanguinet.
Dubrule Lane, off 35 Versailles.
Dufaux, off 159 St. Elizabeth.
Dufferin, off 85 Rachel.
Dufferin Ave., off 439 Richmond.
Dufresne, off 689 Notre Dame.
Duke, off 97 Wellington.
Duluth Ave., off 758 Amherst.
Dumarais, off 151 Cadieux.
Dupre, off 1935 Notre Dame.
Duquette Lane, off 91 Versailles.

Favard, off 88 Sebastopol.
Durocher, off 735 Sherbrooke.
Edgehill Ave., off 1160 Dorchester.
Edinburgh, now Coleraine.
Eleanor, off 266 William.
Elizabeth Terrace, off 25 St. Elizabeth.
Emile, near Arcade.
Erie, off 45 Shaw.
Ernest, off 532 St. Denis.
Esplanade Ave., from Duluth Ave.
Essex Ave., off 1265 Dorchester.
Evans, off 295 St. Urbain.
Evans Lane, from 3 Evans.
Farm, off 425 Wellington.
Forfar, off 67 St. Etienne.
Forgue Ave., off 183 Guy.
Forsythe, off 294 Iberville.
Fortier, off 381 St. Lawrence.
Fortification Lane, off 76 St. Gabriel.
Fortune, off 715 Wellington.
Foundling, off 52 McGill.
Fournier, off 392 Seigneurs.
Friponne, off 64 St. Paul.
Frontenac, off 603 Notre Dame.
Frontenac Lane, off 55 Frontenac.
Fulford, off 384 St. Antoine.
Fullum, off 775 Notre Dame.
Fullum Lane, off 394 Fullum.
Gain, off 975 Notre Dame.
German, now City Hall Avenue.
Gosford, off 401 Craig.
Grand Trunk Street, off 10 Conde.
Grant, off 1272 Notre Dame.
Grant Lane, off 36 Dufresne.
Grey Nun, off 12 William.
Grothe, off 1236 Mignonne.
Groulx Lane, off 63 Versailles.
Guilbault, off 585 St. Lawrence.
Guy, off 2582 St. Catherine.
Guy Ave., off 157 Guy.
Hanover, off 824 Dorchester.
Harbour, off 550 Notre Dame.
Harmony, off Amity, near Fullum.
Hermine, off 764 Craig.
Hibernia, off 845 Wellington.
Hochelaga Market, at Desery Street.
Hospital, off 78 St. Francois Xavier.
Houle, off 337 Wolfe.
Hudson, off 21 Desery.
Hunter, off 12 Canning.
Hutchison, off 707 Sherbrooke.
Iberville, off 621 Notre Dame.
Imperial Ave., off 652 St. James.
Inspector, off 66 St. Antoine.
Island, off 226 St. Patrick.
Jacques Cartier, off 1330 Notre Dame.

Mount St. Mary Ave., off 271 St. Antoine.
Mullins, off 489 Wellington.
Munro, off 24 Champlain.
Murray, off 2130 Notre Dame.
Napoleon, off 728 St. Lawrence.
Napoleon Road, Charlevoix.
Nazareth, off 130 Wellington.
Nillada, off 195 Dufresne.
Nonancourt, off 312 Panet.
Nonancourt, off 241 Papineau Road.
Normand, off 4 Foundling.
Notre Dame, leading street from east to west.
Notre Dame de Lourdes, off 403 Dorchester.
O'Leary Ave., from Railway Track.
Olier, off 31 McCord.
Ontario, off 237 Bleury.
Osborne, from 118 Cathedral.
Oscar Lane, off St. Chas. Borrommee
Ottawa, from 98 Queen.
Overdale Ave., off 372 Aqueduct.
Oxenden Ave., off 317 Prince Arthur.
Palace, off Lagauchetiere, west of Beaver Hall Hill.
Panet Place Lane, off 80 Panet.
Panet, off 1148 Notre Dame.
Panet, St. Jean Baptiste Ward, now Lasalle.
Pantaleon, off 328 Duluth Ave.
Pantaleon, in rear of 110 Laval Ave.
Papineau Road, off Papineau Square.
Papineau Square, off 1080 Notre Dame.
Paris, from 251 Charron.
Park Ave., from north end of Bleury.
Parker, off 356 Visitation.
Parthenais, off 815 Notre Dame.
Parthenais Square, now Parthenais Street.
Paterson, off 218 Delorimier Ave.
Paxton Ave., off 305 Richmond.
Payette, off 29 Chatham.
Pea Lane, off 11 Roy Lane.
Peel, continuation of Windsor, from Dominion Square.
Peel Ave., in rear of 175 Peel.
Perrault Court, now St. Agathe.
Perrault Lane, off 371 Craig.
Perthius, off 27 Campeau.
Phillips Place, between Beaver Hall Square and Phillips Square.
Phillips Square, at 2192 St. Catherine.
Picard Lane, off 1721 St. Catherine.
Pichette, off 266 Barre Lane.

Pine Ave., off 604 St. Lawrence.
Place d'Armes, off 1704 Notre Dame
Place d'Armes Hill, off 101 St. James.
Place Royale, (old Custom House Square), off 460 St. Paul.
Plateau, off 31 Mance.
Plateau Ave, 1990 St. Catherine.
Platt, off 1791 Ontario.
Plessis, off 1333 St. Catherine.
Plymouth Grove, in rear of 385 St. Antoine.
Poele Lane, now Taillefer Ave.
Port, off 10 Common.
Poupart, off 637 Notre Dame.
Prefontaine, off 295 Notre Dame.
Prieur Lane, off 521 Seigneurs.
Prince, off 73 Wellington.
Prince Arthur, off 526 St. Lawrence.
Prince George Ave., off 280 Fullum.
Provencal Lane, off 142 Dufresne.
Providence, off 1181 Mignonne.
Provost, off 117 Descry.
Queen, off 54 Wellington.
Quesnel, off 114 Fulford.
Rachel, off 1071 St. Lawrence.
Railway Track, west from G.T.R. Depot, along the track.
Rapallo, off 303 Craig.
Recollet, off 207 McGill.
Redpath, off 1059 Sherbrooke.
Richardson, off Richmond, south of the canal.
Richmond, off 505 St. James.
Richmond Ave., off 29 Richmond Sq.
Richmond Square, off 308 St. Antoine.
Rivard, off 230 Duluth Ave.
Riverside, off Conway.
Rivet, off 40 Fullum.
Robb, off 95 Poupart.
Robillard, off 114 Moreau.
Robin, off 250 Visitation.
Rolland, off 37 Mountain.
Ropery, off 264 Centre.
Rosario, now Ash Ave.
Rousseau, off 14 Champlain.
Rouville, formerly Mignonne, off 222 St. Michel.
Roy, off 629 St. Lawrence.
Roy Lane, off 1515 Notre Dame.
Rosel, off 107 Hibernia.
Rushbrook, off 123 Hibernia.
Rutherford Ave., off 17 Drummond.
Ryde, off 55 Hibernia.
Sanguinet, off 401 Craig.
School House, formerly St. Philippe, off 19 Mountain.
Scotland, see Argyle Ave.

Seaton, north from Rachel.

Seaton, see Champlain.

Seaver, off 16 Robillard.

Sebastopol, off 576 Wellington.

Seigneurs, off 244 St. Antoine.

Seminary, off 164 McCord.

Seymour Ave., off 1222 Dorchester.

Shannon, off 297 Wellington.

Shaw, off 959 Notre Dame.

Shearer, off 168 Centre.

Sherbrooke, a leading street from east to west, above St. Catherine.

Shuter, off 757 Sherbrooke.

Simpson, off 1094 Sherbrooke.

Smith, off 41 McCord.

Soulanges, formerly St. Henry, off 291 Grand Trunk.

Spiers' Lane, off 162 Prince.

St. Adolphus, off 1016 Notre Dame.

Ste. Agathe, off 28 Cadieux.

St. Agnes, off 6 Farm.

St. Albert, now Chateauguay.

St. Alexander, off 713 Craig.

St. Alexis, off 49 St. Sacrement.

St. Alexis, off 59 Poupart.

St. Alphonse, off 1316 St. Catherine.

St. Amable, off 18 Jacque Cartier Sq.

St. Andre, off 1570 St. Catherine.

St. Andre Lane, off 145 St. Andre.

St. Andrew's now Laprairie.

St. Ann's Market, off 92 McGill.

St. Antoine, continuation of Craig.

St. Antoine Market, cor. Mountain and St. James.

St. Augustin, off 125 McCord.

St. Bernard, off 101 Bleury.

St. Bonaventure, now part of St. James.

St. Catherine, leading street, east to west, between Sherbrooke and Dorchester.

St. Charles, off 779 Charlevoix.

St. Charles Borromee, off 521 Craig.

St. Christophe, off 1692 St. Catherine.

St. Christophe, off 59 Cherrier.

St. Claude, off 1518 Notre Dame.

St. Columban, off 331 Wellington.

St. Constant, now part of Cadieux.

St. Cuthbert, off 671 St. Lawrence.

St. David's Lane, formerly St. Edward, off 1918 Notre Dame.

St. David's Place, at 17 St. David's Lane.

St. Denis, off 363 Craig.

St. Denis Lane, near cor. Mignonne and St. Denis.

St. Dizier, off 167 Commissioner.

St. Dominique, off 483 Craig.

St. Edward, off 165 Bleury.

St. Elizabeth, off 429 Craig.

St. Elizabeth Lane, off 104 Dufresne.

St. Eloi, off 449 St. Paul.

St. Emery, off 176 St. Denis.

St. Etienne, off 396 Wellington.

St. Famille, off 629 Sherbrooke.

St. Felix, off 2180 Notre Dame.

St. Francois, off Barrack.

St. Francois Xavier, off 600 Craig.

St. Gabriel, off 486 Craig.

St. Gabriel Market, cor. Centre and Richmond.

St. Genevieve, off 19 St. Antoine.

St. George, off 2064 St. Catherine.

St. Germain, off 55 Mignonne.

St. Helen, off 1815 Notre Dame.

St. Henry, off 1866 Notre Dame.

St. Henry, now Soulanges.

St. Hubert, off 1650 St. Catherine.

St. Hypolite, off 500 Sherbrooke.

St. Hypolite Lane, off 1610 Ontario.

St. Ignace, off 1671 Notre Dame.

St. James, a leading street from the Court House, west below Craig and St. Antoine.

St. James Market, at 1273 Ontario.

St. Jean Baptiste, now Duluth Ave.

St. Jean Baptiste, off 1606 Notre Dame.

St. Jean Baptiste Market, at 1907 St. Lawrence.

St. John, off 168 St. James.

St. Joseph, now called Notre Dame.

St. Julie, off 88 St. Denis.

St. Justin, off 1876 St. Catherine.

St. Lambert, off 1650 Notre Dame.

St. Lawrence, from 509 Craig.

St. Lawrence Market, at 181 St. Lawrence.

St. Leon Lane, at 21 Rotland Lane.

St. Louis, off 1 St. Hubert.

St. Luke, off 468 Guy.

St. Margaret, off 566 St. James.

St. Mark off 270 St. Catherine.

St. Martin, off 224 St. Antoine.

St. Mary, now called Notre Dame.

St. Matthew, off 2061 St. Catherine.

St. Maurice, off 170 McGill.

St. Michael's Lane, off 1875 Notre Dame.

St. Monique, off 47 St. Antoine.

St. Monique Ave., off 10 St. Monique.

St. Nicholas, off 461 St. Paul.

St. Patrick, off 297 Wellington.

St. Paul, from Dalhousie Square west below Notre Dame.

St. Peter, off 672 Craig.
St. Philip, off 1008 St. Catharine.
St. Pierre Lane, off 587 Mignonne.
St. Raymond, formerly Galen, off 863 Notre Dame.
St. Roch, off 68 Dufresne.
St. Rose, off 133 Visitation.
St. Sacrament, off 75 St. Peter.
St. Sophie, off 748 Craig.
St. Sulpice, off 1702 Notre Dame.
St. Therese, off 72 St. Gabriel.
St. Thomas, off 320 William.
St. Urbain, off 551 Craig.
St. Vincent, off 1576 Notre Dame.
Stadacona, off 112 Marlborough.
Stanley, off 2428 St. Catherine.
Summerhill Ave., off 21 Cote des Neiges Road.
Sussex, off 1257 Dorchester.
Suzanne, now part of Poupart.
Sydenham Lane, off 44 Maisonneuve.
Taillefer Ave., formerly Poete Lane, at 11 Rolland Lane.
Tansley, off 100 Delorimier Ave.
Tar Lane, off 129 Nazareth.
Tara Hall Ave., off St. Urbain Street.
Theatre Lane, off 158 Vitre.
Thistle Terrace, off 128 St. Monique.
Torrance, off 126 Mountain.
Tower Ave., off 2723 St. Catherine
Trudel Lane, off 334 Richmond.

Tupper, off St. Matthew.
Union Ave., off 2178 St. Catherine.
University, off 2208 St. Catherine.
Upper St. Charles Borrommee, off 436 St. Lawrence.
Vallee, off 211 St. George.
Vaudreuil, off 365 St. Paul. .
Versailles, off 248 St. Antoine.
Victor, off 93 St. Paul.
Victoria, off 2264 St. Catherine.
Victoria Square, between McGill and Beaver Hall Hill.
Viger Square, at corner of Craig and St. Denis.
Visitation, off 1183 Notre Dame.
Vitre, off 14 St. Denis.
Voltigeurs, off 1645 Notre Dame.
Water, off lower end of Jacques Cartier.
Wellington, off 52 McGill.
White's Lane, off 123 Vitre.
Widow's Lane, off 39 St. Rose.
William, off 92 McGill.
Windsor, off 602 St. James.
Winning, at 4 Plateau.
Wolfe, off 1280 Notre Dame.
Woodyard, off 1358 Notre Dame.
Workman, off 56 Canning.
Wrexham Ave., off 249 Guy.
Young, off 239 Wellington.
Youville, off 29 McGill.

VICTORIA SQUARE AND QUEEN'S MONUMENT.

FIRE ALARM.

3 General Hospital, Dorchester.
12 Central Fire Station, Craig.
13 General Hospital, Dorchester.
14 Vitre and Sanguinet.
15 Lagauchetiere and St. Lawrence.
16 Dorchester and St. Urbain.
17 Dorchester and Bleury.
18 Beaver Hall and Lagauchetiere.
19 Craig and Little St. Antoine.
21 Dorchester and Union Avenue.
22 Aqueduct and Overdale Ave.
23 No. 5 Fire Station, St. Catherine.
24 St. Catherine and St. Lawrence.
25 St. Elizabeth and Dorchester.
26 St. Catherine and St. Denis.
27 No. 6 Fire Station, Ontario and Avenue de l'Hotel de Ville.
28 Sherbrooke and St. Lawrence.
29 Mance and Sherbrooke.
31 Sherbrooke and University.
32 St. Catherine and McGill College Ave.
33 St. Denis and Dorchester.
34 Charbonneau and St. Lawrence.
35 Shuter and Prince Arthur.
36 King and Common.
37 Duke and Ottawa.
38 Dupre and Notre Dame.
39 St. Antoine and Cathedral.
41 No. 4 Fire Station, Chaboilles Sq.
42 No. 3 Fire Station, Wellington and Dalhousie.
43 Ogilvie's Mills, Mill.
44 Tupper and Sussex.
45 Wellington and McCord.
46 Ottawa and Colborne.
47 McCord and Notre Dame.
48 Mountain and St. Antoine.
49 St. Catherine and Drummond.
51 Sherbrooke and Peel.
52 Guy and St. Antoine.
53 St. Martin and St. James.
54 Notre Dame and Canning.
55 Chatham and St. Antoine.
56 Courcol and Fulford.
57 Seigneurs and William.
58 No. 10 Fire Station, St. Catherine, near Guy.
59 Grey Nunnery, Guy.
61 Canada Sugar Refining Co.
62 No. 9 Fire Station, St. Gabl Mkt.
63 G.T.R. Works, Point St. Charles.
64 Craig and St. Andre.
65 Notre Dame and St. Ignace.
66 Dorchester and Visitation.
67 Notre Dame and Wolfe.

68 Roy and Drolet.
69 Sherbrooke and St. Denis.
71 Dorchester and Crescent.
72 Visitation and Craig.
73 Prince Arthur and Cadieux.
74 St. Andre and Dorchester.
75 St. Christophe and De Montigny.
76 No. 11 Fire Station, Ontario and Beaudry.
77 Amherst and Robin.
78 St. Patrick, opposite Seigneurs.
79 Ogilvie's Mills, Seigneurs.
81 Visitation and Robin.
82 St. Catherine and Panet.
83 Maisonneuve and Dorchester.
84 Logan and Champlain.
85 Champlain and Ontario.
86 Wellington and Congregation.
87 Menai and Forfar.
91 No. 8 Fire Station, Craig and Gain.
92 Notre Dame and Fullum.
93 Ontario and Fullum.
94 Berri and Lagauchetiere.
95 Montreal Gas Works, East End.
96 Montreal Rolling Mills.
97 Shedden Co.'s Stables, William.
112 Notre Dame East, opp. Rolland's.
113 Notre Dame and Gale.
114 No. 13 Fire Station, Desery.
115 Notre Dame, opposite Moreau.
116 Ontario and Moreau.
117 Marlborough and Stadacona.
118 Frontenac and Notre Dame.
119 Iberville and Logan.
121 Parthenais and St. Catharine.
122 C.P.R. Elevator, Dalhousie Sq.
123 Wolfe and Lagauchetiere.
124 Dufresne and De Montigny.
125 St. Christophe and Ontario.
126 St. Etienne and Wellington.
127 Cherrier and St. Hubert.
128 St. Catherine and Amherst.
129 Macdonald's Tobacco Works.
131 Eastern Abattoir.
132 St. Paul, opposite Dupre.
133 St. Catherine and Papineau Road.
134 William and Dalhousie.
135 McCord and Seminary.
136 William and Guy.
137 Notre Dame and Versailles.
138 St. James and Versailles.
139 C.P.R. Shops, Delorimier Ave.
141 St. James and Windsor.
142 No. 12 Fire Station, Seigneurs.
143 Notre Dame, near Guy.
144 Simpson and MacGregor.

145 McTavish Street Reservoir.
146 St. Catherine and Davidson.
147 C.P.R. Workshops, Hochelaga.
148 Papineau Road, opposite St. Rose.
149 Canada Rubber Works, Notre Dame.
151 St. Monique and Lagauchetiere.
152 Mansfield and Dorchester.
153 St. Catherine and Fort.
154 Windsor and Osborne.
155 Dorchester and St. Mark.
156 Sherbrooke and Mackay.
157 Ontario and St. Urbain.
158 Mantha's Mill, St. Charles Borromere.
159 Civic Hospital, head of Moreau.
161 Wellington and Hibernia.
162 No. 15 Fire Station, Hibernia.
163 Centre and Island.
164 Centre and Ropery.
165 Wheelhouse, Water Works.
166 Knox and Charlevoix.
167 Wellington and Charron.
168 Cor. Leber and Bourgeois.
169 St. Catherine and Fulham, Providence Convent.
171 St. Patrick and Charlevoix.
172 St. Patrick and Laprairie.
173 Magdalen and Favard.
174 Exchange Hotel, Mill.
175 Centre and Charlevoix.
176 Grand Trunk and Shearer.
177 G.T.R. Stockyard, St. Etienne.
211 St. Hypolite and Roy.
212 Napoleon and Cadieux.
213 Duluth and St. Lawrence.
214 Duluth and St. Denis.
215 Sanguinet and Rachel.
216 No. 14 Fire Station, St. Dominique.
217 St. Lawrence, opposite Marie Anne.
218 Avenue de l'Hotel de Ville and Marie Anne.
219 Cadieux and Mount Royal Ave.
221 St. Andre near Duluth.
222 No. 16 Fire Station, Rachel.
223 Dufferin and Mount Royal Ave.
224 Exhibition Grounds.
225 Park and Milton Avenues.
226 Rachel and Seaton.
227 Sherbrooke and Shaw.
228 Hotel Dieu Hospital.
229 St. Urbain and Prince Arthur.
231 St. Paul, opposite Friponne.
232 St. Louis and Berri.
233 No. 7 Fire Station, Dalhousie Sq.

234 Craig and Bonsecours.
235 Windsor Hotel.
236 Cote and Vitre.
237 De Montigny and Cadieux.
241 Bonsecours and Notre Dame.
242 St. Claude and St. Paul.
243 Court House, Notre Dame.
244 Notre Dame Hospital.
245 St. Denis and Carrieres.
446 No. 17 Fire Station, St. Denis.
247 Carrieres and St. Joseph.
248 Rivard and Perreault.
249 Deaf and Dumb Institute, St. Denis.
251 No. 2 Fire Station, St. Gabriel.
252 Roy and St. Hubert.
253 Rivard and Rachel.
254 Rivard and Marie Anne.
255 McGill College.
256 Grand Seminary, Sherbrooke.
257 Mount St. Mary Convent, Guy.
258 Boys' Home, Mountain.
259 Philosophical Seminary, Cote des Neiges.
261 Mount Royal Ave. and Berri.
262 Marie Anne and LaSalle.
263 St. Hubert and Belanger.
264 Oil Works, Mile End.
265 St. Zotique and St. Hubert.
266 Labelle and Beaubien.
271 Academy St. Louis de Gonzague, Sherbrooke.
272 Good Shepherd Convent, 500 Sherbrooke.
273 Emily and Cuthbert.
274 Breboeuf and Gilford.
275 Amherst, near St. Zotique, 18 Fire Station.
281 St. Hubert and Fleurimont.
282 St. Hubert and Comte.
312 Jacques Cartier Sq. and St. Paul.
313 St. Paul and St. Jean Baptiste.
314 Notre Dame, op. St. Lambert Hill.
315 Craig and St. Lambert Hill.
316 Dorchester and Shaw.
317 St. Catherine and St. Hubert.
318 St. Catherine and Avenue de l'Hotel de Ville.
319 St. Catherine and Providence Convent.
321 St. James and Place d'Armes.
322 St. Sulpice and Le Royer.
324 Place Royale and St. Paul.
331 Sanguinet and DeMontigny.
332 St. Denis and Ontario.
333 Reformatory Prison, DeMontigny.
324 Sherbrooke and Amherst.

341 St. Francois Xavier, opp. St. Sacrament.
342 St. Frs. Xavier and Notre Dame.
343 St. James and St. Peter.
344 Fortification and St. George.
351 Craig, opp. St. Alexander.
352 Recollet and St. Helen.
372 Bishop's Palace, Lagauchetiere.
373 Little Sisters of the Poor, Seigneurs.
374 Ladies' Benevolent Society, Berthelet.
375 Sacred Heart Convent, St. Alexander.
376 Western Hospital.
412 St. James, op. St. Michael's Lane.
413 McGill and Notre Dame.
414 St. Henry and St. Maurice.
415 St. Sacrament and St. Peter.
421 McGill and St. Paul.
423 Foundling and Port.
424 Dalhousie and Common.
425 Dom. Transport Co.'s stable, Ann.
431 Youville and St. Peter.
432 Grey Nun and Wellington.
433 Mill Street, near Black's Bridge.
511 Lagauchetiere and St. George.
512 St. Catherine and St. Philip.
513 Ontario and Bleury.

514 Berthelet and Aylmer.
515 Sherbrooke and Mountain.
516 St. Catherine and Bishop.
517 St. Luke and St. Mark.
518 Albert and Canning.
519 Notre Dame and Murray.
521 William and Young.
522 Conde and St. Patrick.
523 Lafontaine and Plessis.
524 Montcalm and DeMontigny.
525 Desery and Stadacona.
526 Poupart and St. Catharine.
527 DeMontigny and Plessis.
528 Avenue de l'Hotel de Ville and Lagauchetiere.
529 East End Electric Station, Water.
531 Delorimier Ave., and Lafontaine.
532 Delorimier and Ontario.
533 Shaw and DeMontigny.
534 Singer Manufacturing Co., Notre Dame,
535 Mount St. Louis Institute, Sherbrooke.
536 Poisy's Piano Factory, Papineau Ave.
537 Victoria Hospital.
538 C.P.R. Workshops, Hochelaga.
541 Female Prison.
542 Cotton Factory, Hochelaga.

CONSULATES AND VICE-CONSULATES.

Argentine Confederation, F. C. Henshaw, consul ; F. L. Wanklyn, vice-consul, Montreal Street Railway Chambers, Place d'Armes Hill.

Austro-Hungarian, Ed. Schultze, consul-general; 166 McGill.

Belgian, Jesse Joseph, consul, 180 St. James; P. H. Mathys, vice-consul, 301 St. James.

Chili, George B. Day, consul-general, Imperial bldg, 107 St. James.

Danish, Herman H. Wolff, 170 McGill.

French consul-general, A. Kieczkowski, 99 St. James; consul charge de la chancellerie, L. Duchastel de Montrouge; attache, vicomte R. de Saint Phalle.

German Empire, Franz Bopp, LL.D., consul, 690 Sherbrooke.

Greece, J. Ponsonby Sexton, consul-general.

Italy, Com. G. Solimbergo, Royal consul-general for Canada, in Montreal: J. Internoscia, M.A., B.C.L., attache to the consulate, 97 St. James; chevalier A. M. F. Gianelli, honorary consul, Toronto; vice-consuls, at Quebec and Toronto and consular agent at Victoria, B.C.

Netherlands, Karel D. W. Boissevain, consul-general, 301 St. James:

S. B. Howard, vice-consul, 39 St. Sacrament.

Portugal, F. R. Routh, consul, 195 Commissioners.

Consulat Imperial de Russie, Nicolas de Struve, Imperial consul, hours 10 a.m. to 1 p.m., 50 Durocher.

Sweden and Norway, Gustaf Gylling, vice-consul, 18 St. Alexis.

Switzerland, D. L. Rey, consul, 14 Cadieux; Ed. Sandreuter, vice-consul, Board of Trade Bldg., St. Sacrament.

Republic of Uruguay, Fred. C. Henshaw, vice-consul, Mont. St. Ry. Chambers, Place d'Armes Hill.

Spanish, Senor Don Hipolito de Uriarte Iladia, consul-general ; Don Rafael de Casares, vice-consul, office 207 St. James.

United States consul-general for Province of Quebec, John L. Bittinger; vice and deputy consul-general, P. Gorman, 260 St. James.

United States of Mexico, D. A. Ansell, consul-general, for Dominion of Canada, 39 St. Sacrament.

United States of Columbia, Rodolpho Lemieux, consul, 1592 Notre Dame.

Monaco, J. L. Coutlee, consul, Imperial bldg , 107 St. James.

A Gentleman Barber.

Few men are better known among the West End gentry than MR. THOMAS SUTTON, who keeps the Hair Dressing Parlors at 134 Peel Street. For over twenty years, MR. SUTTON has been in business on the same street within a couple of blocks of his present quarters. Besides understanding his business thoroughly, MR. SUTTON can discuss the most important subjects of the day in a manner that can be excelled by few. His comparisons are often very original. The author, for many years has made it a point to consult MR. SUTTON on very important mental problems.

ALPHABETICAL LIST OF THE CHARTERED BANKS OF CANADA, AND THEIR HEAD OFFICES.

Bank of British Columbia, London, Eng.
Bank of British North America, London, Eng.
Bank of Hamilton, Hamilton, Ont.
Bank of Montreal, Montreal, Que.
Bank of New Brunswick, St. John, N.B.
Bank of Nova Scotia, Halifax, N.S.
Bank of Ottawa, Ottawa, Ont.
Bank of Toronto, Toronto, Ont.
Bank of Yarmouth, Yarmouth, N.S.
Banque d'Hochelaga, Montreal, Que.
Banque de St-Jean, St. Johns, Que.
Banque Nationale, Quebec, Que.
Banque de St. Hyacinthe, St. Hyacinthe, Que.
Canadian Bank of Commerce, Toronto, Ont.
Commercial Bank of Windsor, Windsor, Ont.
Dominion Bank, Toronto, Ont.
Eastern Townships Bank, Sherbrooke, Que.

Exchange Bank of Yarmouth, Yarmouth, N.S.
Halifax Banking Co., Halifax, N.S.
Imperial Bank of Canada, Toronto, Ont.
Merchant's Bank of Canada, Montreal, Que.
Merchants' Bank of Halifax, Halifax, N.S.
Merchants Bank of P.E.I., Charlottetown, P.E.I.
Molson's Bank, Montreal, Que.
Ontario Bank, Toronto, Ont.
People's Bank of Halifax, N.S.
People's Bank, New Brunswick.
Quebec Bank, Montreal, Que.
Standard Bank of Canada, Toronto, Ont.
St. Stephens Bank, St. Stephens, N.B.
Summerside Bank, Summerside, P.E.I.
Traders Bank of Canada, Toronto, Ont.
Union Bank of Canada, Montreal, Que.
Union Bank of Halifax, Halifax, N.S.
Western Bank of Canada, Oshawa, Ont.

NORMAN MURRAY,

Book, News and Advertising Agent.

PUBLISHER OF

"Murray's Illustrated Guide to Montreal,"

"Murray's Broadsides," Etc., Etc. . . . .

21 BEAVER HALL HILL, MONTREAL.

FAILED BANKS AND BANKS IN LIQUIDATION.

Agricultural Bank of Upper Canada..	Worthless.
Bank of Acadia, Nova Scotia	Do.
Bank of Brantford, Ont.	Do.
Bank of Canada, Montreal	Do.
Bank of Clifton	Do.
Bank of Liverpool, Nova Scotia, September, 1870.	Do.
Bank of Prince Edward Island, June, 1882	Do.
Bank of London, closed July, 1887	Do.
Bank of Upper Canada	Refuse.
Banque Ville Marie	Worthless.
Banque Jacques Cartier	Do.
Central Bank of Canada, Toronto, Ont., closed Oct., 1887.	Worthless.
Central Bank of New Brunswick, Fredericton, closed 1882	Do.
City Bank of Montreal	Do.
Colonial Bank of Canada, Toronto.	Do.
Commercial Bank of New Brunswick, July, 1868	Do.
Commercial Bank of Manitoba, Winnipeg	98 cents.
Commercial Bank of Newfoundland	Refuse.
Consolidated Bank of Montreal, since May 7, 1890	Worthless.
Exchange Bank of Canada, Montreal, August, 1883	Do.
Farmers' Bank of Rustico, P.E.I.	Refuse.
Farmers' Bank of Toronto, Ont.	Worthless.
Federal Bank of Canada, since May 4, 1893	Do.
International Bank of Canada, Toronto, closed 1865.	Do.
La Banque du Peuple, Montreal	Refuse.
Maritime Bank, St. John, N.B.	Do.
Mechanics' Bank of Montreal, August, 1879	Worthless.
Mechanics' Bank of St. John	Do.
Pictou Bank, closed May, 1887.	95 cents.
Royal Canadian Bank of Montreal	Worthless.
Stadacona Bank of Quebec, since April 29, 1890	Do.
The Bank of Western Canada	Do.
Union Bank of Newfoundland	Refuse.
Westmorland Bank of New Brunswick	Worthless.
Zimmerman's Bank, 1858	Do.

Notes are raised from a smaller denomination to a higher in various ways : 1st, the figures in the counters are extracted with a powerful acid, and figures of a larger denomination are printed in their places. This can be easily detected, as the letters and figures substituted are of an inferior quality to that on the balance of the note. 2nd, counters are torn from genuine notes and substituted for those extracted. This is known as the pasting process. The alterations can be readily detected by holding the note to the light, which will at once disclose the parts pasted on.

CHRONOLOGY OF CANADA (Condensed).

1492—Columbus discovers the islands of America.

1497—Cabot discovers the mainland.

1517—Cabot visits Hudson's Bay.

1535—Jacques Cartier ascends the St. Lawrence, (August 10).

1541-43—First attempts at settlement (unsuccessful).

1598—Forty Convicts left on Sable Island, only twelve of whom were found alive five years afterwards.

1603—Champlain's first visit.

1605—Port Royal (Annapolis) founded.

1608—Second visit of Champlain. Foundation of Quebec, the first permanent settlement of Canada.

1613—Foundation of St. John's, Newfoundland.

1625—Jesuits arrive at Quebec.

1629—Quebec taken by the British.

1632—Canada and Acadia restored to France.

1642—Ville Marie (Montreal) founded by Maisonneuve.

1654—Acadia taken by the British.

1667—Acadia restored to France.

1670—Hudson's Bay Co. founded.

1672—Frontenac appointed Gov. of Canada (white population about 6,700.)

1689—Massacre of Lachine.

1690—Sir W. Phipps captures Port Royal.

1713—Acadia (Nova Scotia) Hudson Bay Territory, and Newfoundland ceded to Britain.

1739—Population of Canada 42,700.

1745—Louisbourg taken by the New Englanders.

1748—Louisbourg restored to France.

1749—Halifax founded.

1755—Expulsion of Acadians from Nova Scotia.

1758—Louisbourg recaptured by the British.

1759—British under Wolf defeat the French under Montcalm on the Plains of Abraham, Quebec.

1760—Canada (population 70,000) surrenders to Britain.

1774—"Quebec Act" passed, giving the French-Canadians the free exercise of the R. C. religion, and their own civil laws and customs, and providing for the administration of the criminal law as used in England and the appointment of a Legislative Council by the Crown.

1775—Outbreak of the American Revolution and invasion of Canada by the Americans, capture of Montreal and unsuccessful attack on Quebec.

1776—Americans driven out of Canada.

1783—Second Treaty of Paris and definition of boundary between United States and Canada. Foundation of St. John, N.B., by U. E. Loyalists. Population of Canada about 165,000.

1784—New Brunswick made a separate province.

1791—Passage of Canadian Act, dividing Canada into Upper and Lower Canada.

1792—First meeting of the Parliaments, of Upper Canada at Newark or Niagara, and Lower Canada at Quebec.

1793—Slavery abolished in Upper Canada.

1794—Toronto, then called York, founded, and is made capital of Upper Canada in 1796.

1806—Population of Lower Canada 250,000, and Upper Canada 70,718.

1812—War between Great Britain and United States. Detroit captured by the Canadians (Aug. 11). Battle of Queenston Heights (Oct. 13).

1813—Toronto captured and burned by the Americans (April. 25). Battles of Stony Creek (June 5), Moraviantown (Sept.), Chateauguay (Oct. 26), and Chrysler's Farm (Nov. 11.)

1814—Americans defeated at Lundy's Lane (July 25). War ended by the treaty of Ghent (Dec. 24). Population of Lower Canada 335,000 and of Upper Canada 95,000.

1831—Population of Lower Canada 553,134 and of Upper Canada. 236,702.

1836—Opening of the first railway in Canada between Laprairie and St. Johns.

1837-8—Rebellion of Mackenzie and Papineau.

1841—Reunion of Upper and Lower Canada and responsible government established. First joint Parliament meets at Kingston (June 13). Population of Lower Canada 690,000, and of Upper Canada, 455,000.

1849—See Montreal Chronology.

1851—Population of Lower Canada 890,264; of Upper Canada, 952,004; of New Brunswick, 193,800; of Nova Scotia, 276,854.

1852—Commencement of the Grand Trunk Railway.

1858—Ottawa made Capital of Canada. Decimal system of currency adopted.

1861—Population of Upper Canada, 1,396,091; of Lower Canada, 1,111,566; of New Brunswick, 252,147; of Nova Scotia, 330,857; of Prince Edward Island, 80,857.

1866—Fenian Invasion of Canada.

1867—The British North America Act passed by the Imperial Legislature, effecting a union of the Provinces of Canada. Nova Scotia and New Brunswick under the name of the Dominion of Canada. The names of Upper and Lower Canada to Ontario and Quebec. Lord Monk is first Governor-General, Sir John A. Macdonald (died 1891) first premier.

1862—First Red River (Riel) Rebellion.

1870—Manitoba admitted to the Confederation.

1871—British Columbia joins Confederation. Total population of the Dominion, 3,635,000.

1873—Prince Edward Island joins the Confederation.

1876—Intercolonial opened from Quebec to Halifax.

1881—Population of the Dominion 4,324,826.

1885—Second Riel Rebellion. C.P.R. completed across the continent.

1891—Population of the Dominion, 4,833,239.

ST. JAMES METHODIST CHURCH.

VERDICT WELL MERITED.

THE acme of perfection and good taste in Gents' wearing apparel is shown in the selection of patterns, which FIT REFORM import each season. They are **Nobby, Genteel** and yet **Quiet.**

Throughout the breadth of the land in this respect, verdict declares in favor of

FIT REFORM,

2344 St. Catherine Street, Montreal.

AGENCIES AT

Vancouver, B.C.	Brockville, O.	Fredericton, N.B.
Victoria, B.C.	St. Thomas, O.	Woodstock, N.B.
Ottawa, O.	Picton, O.	Halifax, N.S.
London, O.	Orangeville, O.	New Glasgow, N.S.
Guelph, O.	St. John, N.B.	Truro, N.S.
Kingston, O.	St. Stephen, N.B.	Charlottetown, P.E.I.

PARISH CHURCH OF NOTRE DAME.

FOR INSURANCE

OF ALL KINDS, AT LOWEST RATES

APPLY TO————————•

DAVID DENNE,

100 St. Francois Xavier Street, Montreal.

Telephone, Main 220.

INTERIOR NOTRE DAME CHURCH.

BONSECOURS MARKET AND BONSECOURS CHURCH.

Ladies or Gentlemen
Cannot get a Better

Breakfast, Dinner or Supper

Anywhere at any price, than at

Beau's Arcade Café

2336 St. Catherine Street,

For 25 cents.

You get quantity and quality. . . . .
The very best material, cooked by the very
best cooks and served by attentive and
polite waitresses. . . . .

ONE BLOCK FROM DOMINION SQUARE.

ST. PETER'S CATHEDRAL,

Properly speaking, the Cathedral of St. James, Dominion Square.

Tourist and Amateur Photographers

will find a full lot of supplies.

Developing and Printing carefully and promptly done.

❧ ❧ Views of City, Etc. ❧ ❧

❧ ❧ ❧

W. B. BAIKIE,

2257 St. Catherine Street,

MONTREAL.

CHRIST CHURCH CATHEDRAL (Anglican).

ESTABLISHED 1842.

219 St. James Street, MONTREAL.

CONFECTIONERY, COFFEE AND LUNCHEON ROOMS.

Visitors to Montreal will find this a first-Class Dining Room for Ladies and
Gentlemen. Ladies can leave their parcels and hand baggage
here, while doing their shopping in the City.

MANUFACTURER OF

PURE CONFECTIONERY

RETAIL ONLY,

CHAS. M. ALEXANDER, Proprietor.

DOMINION SQUARE AND WINDSOR HOTEL.

ASHFORD'S

Books, Stationery, and Circulating Library.

✿ ✿ ✿ ✿ ✿ ✿ ✿

Guide Books, Unmounted Photos, Views of Montreal, Photos of Royalty and other celebrities.

Standard and Miscellaneous Books. New Books received daily, among them the latest novels and magazines.

Valuable Books at Reduced Prices.

Old and Rare Books relating to the Early History of Canada.

Medical and Surgical Books.

Bibles, Prayer, Hymn and other Devotional Books, both in Cheap and Finest Bindings.

STATIONERY

Of all kinds. The Finest Note Papers and Envelopes, as well as the inferior qualities, such as five quires for 25 cents.

LEATHER GOODS.

Purses, Pocket Books and Writing Cases in all styles. Prices reasonable.

C. ASHFORD,

800 DORCHESTER STREET.

ESTABLISHED IN 1876. *TEL. UP 1342.*

ROYAL VICTORIA HOSPITAL.

OLD ST. GABRIEL PRESBYTERIAN CHURCH.

HENDERSON'S
Souvenir and Book Store

DOMINION SQUARE, (No. 142) just above
the Windsor Hotel.

STERLING SILVER SOUVENIR JEWELLERY.

Album Views of the City, 10c, 40c. 50c and $1 00.

Album Views of Quebec, Thousand Islands, Niagara Falls, &c., &c.

A very complete line of all the new Novels of the day.

The Cheap 10 and 15 cent Novels—very large stock.

◆ INDIAN CURIOS. ◆

Strangers to the City are invited to call.

MONTREAL BIBLE HOUSE,
2175 St. Catherine Street.

Coat of Arms of the Dominion and the Seven Provinces.

ONTARIO. DOMINION. QUEBEC.
NOVA SCOTIA.   NEW BRUNSWICK.
MANITOBA. PRINCE EDWARD ISLAND. BRITISH COLUMBIA.

VICTORIA BRIDGE.

J. E. TREMBLE

FAMILY and

DISPENSING CHEMIST

2480 St. Catherine Street, Corner of Mountain Street.

Telephone, Up Town 910.   (Three blocks west of Dominion Square.)

Established in 1891.

Our Motto: NONE BETTER.

OUR BEST ADVERTISEMENT IS :

1. The Quality and Assortment of our Goods.
2. Style of sending out.
3. Promptness in delivery.

Strangers, Tourists and other Travellers will be treated right.

GIVE US A TRIAL.

The Montreal Book Trade.

This Guide is always for sale at the following Book Stores:

WINDSOR HOTEL NEWS STAND.

W. DRYSDALE & CO., 2478 St. Catherine Street.

G.W. CLARKE & Co., Fancy Goods, etc., 2270 St. Catherine Street.

J. T. HENDERSON, Bookseller and Lending Library,

142 Peel Street.

NORMAN MURRAY, 21 Beaver Hall Hill.

W. FOSTER BROWN, 2323 St. Catherine Street.

ST. LAWRENCE HALL NEWS STAND.

C. ASHFORD, 800 Dorchester Street.

EBEN PICKEN, 33 Beaver Hall Hill.

D. & J. SADLIER, Catholic Publishers and Booksellers,

1669 Notre Dame Street.

F. E. PHELAN, 2331 St. Catherine Street.

JOSEPH FORTIER, 254 St. James Street.

W. B. BAIKIE, 2257 St. Catherine Street.

E. M. RENOUF, 2238 St. Catherine Street.

A. T. CHAPMAN, 2407 St. Catherine Street.

DAVID WATERS, 494 St. James Street.

FRENCH BOOKSELLERS AND PUBLISHERS.

CADIEUX & DEROME, 1603 Notre Dame Street.

GRANGER FRERES, 1190 Notre Dame Street,

opposite Notre Dame Church.

FABRE & GRAVEL, 1619 Notre Dame Street.

YOUNG MEN'S CHRISTIAN ASSOCIATION

THOMAS SONNE,

MANUFACTURER OF

Awnings, Tents, Sails and Flags of all Nations,

WAGGON COVERS, HORSE COVERS.

193 Commissioners St., MONTREAL.

Telephone, Main 1161.

NORMAN MURRAY,

21 BEAVER HALL HILL,

Sells more English Periodicals than any other
dealer in Montreal.

TABLE SHOWING THE CANADIAN CUSTOMS VALUES

OF THE PRINCIPAL FOREIGN CURRENCIES.

COUNTRY.	MONETARY UNIT.	STANDARD.	VALUE IN DOLLARS & CENTS.
Austria	Florin	Silver	$0.37.1
Belgium	Franc	Gold and Silver	.19.3
Bolivia	Dollar	Gold and Silver	.96.5
Brazil	Milreis	Gold	.54.5
Bogota	Peso	Gold	.96.5
Central America	Dollar	Silver	.93.5
Chili	Peso	Gold	.91.2
China	Tael	Silver	1.38.0
Denmark	Crown	Gold	.26.8
Ecuador	Dollar	Silver	.93.5
Egypt	Pound of 1·0 piastres	Gold	4.97.4
France	Franc	Gold and Silver	.19.3
Greece	Drachm	Gold and Silver	.19.3
German Empire	Mark	Gold	.23.8
Japan	Yen	Gold	.59.7
India	Rupee of 16 annas	Silver	.44.4
Italy	Lira	Gold and Silver	.19.3
Liberia	Dollar	Gold	1.00.
Mexico	Dollar	Silver	1.01.5
Netherlands	Florin	Gold and Silver	.38.5
Norway	Crown	Gold	.26.8
Peru	Dollar	Silver	.93.5
Portugal	Milreis	Gold	1.08.
Russia	Rouble	Silver	.74.8
Sandwich Islands	Dollar	Gold	1.00.
Spain	Peseta of 100 centimes	Gold and Silver	.19.3
Sweden	Crown	Gold	.26.8
Switzerland	Franc	Gold and Silver	.19.3
Tripoli	Mahbub of 20 piastres	Silver	.84.4
Turkey	Piaster	Gold	.04.3
United States of Columbia	Peso	Silver	.96.5

PENCE.		SHILLINGS.		SHILLINGS.	
1	2 cents	1	24½ cents	13	$3.16½
2	4	2	48½	14	3.40½
3	6	3	73	15	3.65
4	8	4	97½	16	3.89½
5	10	5	$1.21½	17	4.13½
6	12	6	1.46	18	4.38
7	14	7	1.70½	19	4.62
8	16	8	1.94½	20	4.86½
9	18	9	2.19		
10	20	10	2.43½		
11	22	11	2.67½		
12	24½	12	2.92		

LACHINE RAPIDS

THE STATIONS OF THE CROSS IN THE R. C. CEMETERY

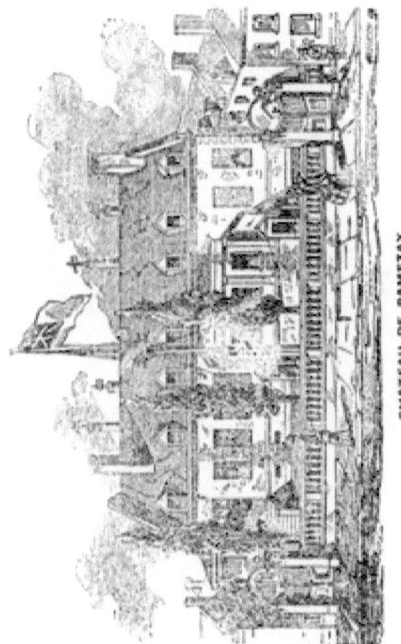

CHATEAU DE RAMEZAY

NELSON'S MONUMENT,
Jacques Cartier Square.

GENERAL VIEW OF McGILL COLLEGE.

For Books you cannot get anywhere
else, try ✄ ✄ ✄ ✄

NORMAN MURRAY,
21 BEAVER HALL HILL.

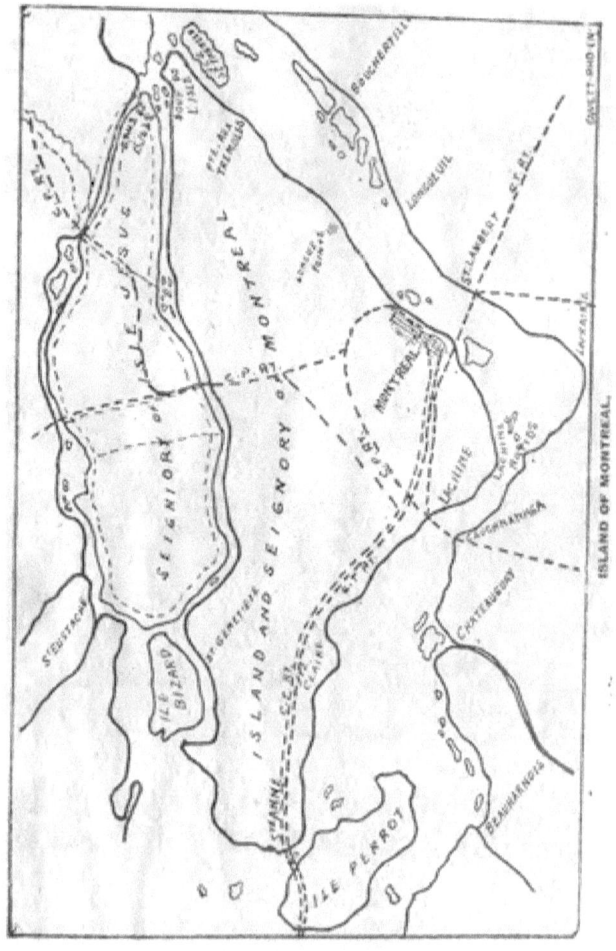

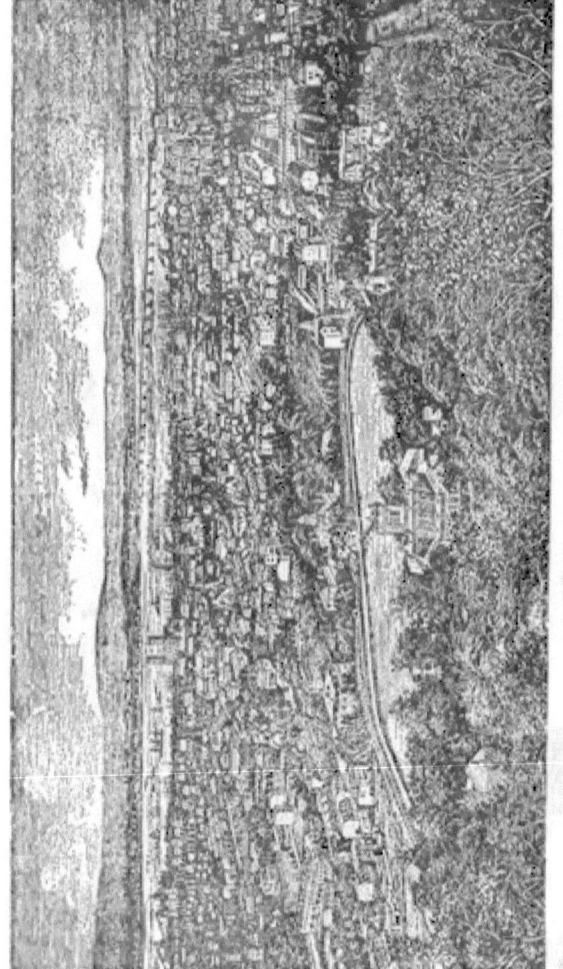

MONTREAL FROM THE MOUNTAIN.